TO DATE OR NOT TO DATE . . .

"I was wondering if you'd like to go to the library with me tomorrow and study for the physics test? We could get a Coke afterwards at the drugstore," Bruce said.

Thinking of Tom, E.E. didn't know what to say. Why, oh, why had Bruce asked her out on the same kind of date? Stalling, she finally said, "I'll have to check on family plans first."

That seemed to satisfy Bruce, who told her he'd call in the evening to check. But, hurrying back to her locker after class, E.E. didn't know what to do, at least not until she overheard Marsha Thompson talking to Tammy.

"As far as I know," Marsha was saying, "you're the first girl Bruce has asked out. Where's he taking you?"

"To a movie, then some place for a hamburger. I can hardly wait," said Tammy.

Slamming her locker, E.E. hurried away. She had her answer. She would tell Bruce after their next class that she had no intention of going anywhere with him, especially not to the library! Bruce Johnson wouldn't have a chance to make a fool out of her . . .

SMART GIRL

The Latest Books from SIGNET VISTA

SMART GIRL

SANDY MILLER

A SIGNET VISTA BOOK
NEW AMERICAN LIBRARY
TIMES MIRROR

PUBLISHED BY
THE NEW AMERICAN LIBRARY
OF CANADA LIMITED

NAL BOOKS ARE AVAILABLE AT QUANTITY DISCOUNTS
WHEN USED TO PROMOTE PRODUCTS OR SERVICES. FOR
INFORMATION PLEASE WRITE TO PREMIUM MARKETING DIVISION,
THE NEW AMERICAN LIBRARY, INC., 1633 BROADWAY,
NEW YORK, NEW YORK 10019.

RL6/IL5+

A special thanks to Aileen Fisher for allowing me to use
part of her poem "Butterfly Wings."

First Printing, November, 1982

2   3   4   5   6   7   8   9

SIGNET VISTA TRADEMARK REG. U.S. PAT. OFF. AND FOREIGN
COUNTRIES REGISTERED TRADEMARK—MARCA REGISTRADA
HECHO EN WINNIPEG, CANADA

SIGNET, SIGNET CLASSICS, MENTOR, PLUME, MERIDIAN
and NAL BOOKS are published in Canada by The New American
Library of Canada, Limited, Scarborough, Ontario

PRINTED IN CANADA
COVER PRINTED IN U.S.A.

*To my parents,
Norman and Beckie Peden,
with love*

BUTTERFLY WINGS

How would it be
on a day in June
to open your eyes
in a dark cocoon,

And soften one end
and crawl outside,
and find you had wings
to open wide . . .

—Aileen Fisher
from *In the Woods, In the
Meadow, In the Sky*

1

Elizabeth Ellen Clark glanced up at the clock on the wall—five minutes after one. She'd better hurry if she was planning to get to her next class on time.

Her eyes wandered over the library as she gathered up the books she had just checked out. It felt great to be back in school, and there was something about any library that she loved. She couldn't put her finger on exactly what it was, maybe just the idea that there was so much knowledge crammed into one place. Even the smell pleased her, kind of a musty, leathery aroma that tickled her nostrils.

It wasn't until she was checking out her books that she noticed them—Tom Martin and Susan Lewis. They were walking out the door hand in hand and he was bending over whispering something in Susan's ear. Elizabeth caught her breath sharply, and a huge lump squeezed in her throat at the mere thought of last spring and Tom Martin, the handsome track star.

How could she have been so naive as to believe that he really liked her? He was the first and only boy to show her any attention. He used to take her to the drugstore for Cokes and then they would go to the library to study.

For someone who was supposed to be the smartest student in the whole school, she had certainly been stupid about Tom. She had no idea he only needed help with his chemistry so he would remain eligible for the track team.

How could she have been so gullible? He dropped her as soon as he was doing better in class, and started dating Susan. She felt certain that she had been the laughingstock of the school for the rest of that year.

Well, she wasn't going to be hurt again. She'd made up her mind—this year she was going to study harder than ever and look out only for herself. She would excel in the one thing she was good at, and never date again. Not that anyone would ask her, anyway.

As soon as her books were ready, Elizabeth opened the one she had been reading and set it on top of the stack. After pushing her horn-rimmed glasses higher on her nose with her right forefinger, she began to scan the page as she walked toward the swinging doors into the hall.

There was a barely perceptible creak when she pushed open the door . . . then, thud! She crashed into someone entering the same door and books flew in every direction at once. Plop! plop! plop! they landed noisily at her feet. She could feel her face growing warm as the sound reverberated through the hall like a small explosion.

"S-sorry," she stammered, as she looked up into a pair of incredibly blue eyes. They belonged to a boy she had never seen in Falls City, Oklahoma before.

"It *would* help if you watched where you're going," he said, softening his words with a grin. "But I guess that's what you call starting the school year off with a bang!" Stooping down, he began picking up books.

Hastily, she bent over to help. "I hope this won't make you late for class," she said, measuring the tone of her voice carefully. Somehow she could never make words come out sounding friendly the way she wanted them to. Not that she wanted to sound *too* friendly.

"We'll make it on time. Here," he said, handing her some books, and reading the titles at the same time. "The biographies of Isaac Newton and Albert Einstein. A girl after my own heart," he said with a big smile.

She took the books, adding them to the trigonometry, physics, and four other books she had retrieved.

"What's your next class?" he asked, straightening his own books.

"Trig."

"Same direction I'm heading. I'll carry part of those for you."

"I can manage." The muscles in her jaw felt tight, and her words sounded stiff and unnatural as she squeezed them out. She really didn't mean them to sound that way at all, but she couldn't seem to help it.

Just then the top book slid off her stack and thudded to the floor once more.

"It doesn't *look* like you can manage," the boy stated, picking up the book. His blue eyes sparkled with good humor as he reached over and grabbed some more of her books, then tucked them under his arm. "We'd better hurry." He started down the hall with long strides, and Elizabeth hurried to catch up with him.

"Really, I can take care of myself," she insisted firmly, drawing herself up to her full five feet seven inches. She still felt small next to this boy. He must be about six feet tall.

"We forgot to introduce ourselves," he said, ignoring her remark. "I'm Bruce Johnson. We just moved here from Okmulgee."

"I'm E.E. Clark." Her brown loafers made a soft click, click on the tile floor as she almost ran to keep up with him.

"E.E.?" Bruce said, running his large hand through his sandy hair and looking at her with a questioning expression.

"My initials, really, but it's what everyone calls me."

"H-m-m," he replied. "So what do they stand for? No, don't tell me. Let me guess first. Let's see, how about Ernestine Esmerelda?" he said, his blue eyes crinkling at the edges as he smiled.

"Even I would die if my folks named me something like that," E.E. answered lightly.

"Engleberta Evangeline?"

"You're getting worse," E.E. said as they stopped

at the door of the math room. "I'll take those now," she said, holding out her hand for her books.

"This is where I turn in, too," Bruce said, handing them to her.

"Oh," E.E. murmured as the last bell clanged noisily.

"Wait, you still haven't told me your name yet."

"Surely you're not going to give up after two guesses," E.E. answered before she stepped through the door.

She noted with relief that there was one empty seat left on the front row. She always liked to sit on the front, and it would give this Bruce guy a good reason to part ways with her.

He was a nice looking boy with his sandy hair and freckles, Elizabeth found herself thinking as she slid into her seat. She liked the confident way he held his broad shoulders, and he had certainly been friendly enough. But then he was new here and didn't know her.

He would find out in time that boys never had anything to do with her. That was okay. She didn't want anything to do with them, either, not after last year. Unbidden tears stung her eyes as she thought about Tom once more. Seeing him with Susan today had brought back all the hurt and humiliation.

E.E. fingered the pony-tail holder that caught her long chestnut hair and fastened it primly at the nape of her neck. Everyone except her best friend, Cindy, seemed to think that she was some sort of computerized wonder without any feelings, and they more or less left her alone. Well, she did have feelings, but it was a lot less painful when you didn't let people know.

Math was one of her favorite subjects and here she was, brooding over things that couldn't be changed. Sitting up straight, she pushed all those unpleasant thoughts to the back of her mind as Mr. Hanover began to call the roll.

Fifty minutes later, E.E. felt as if they were just getting started when it was already time to quit. The bell rang and everyone called greetings to friends they hadn't seen recently.

After saying a few "hi's", E.E. slipped quietly out the door. She would like to say something more, but after "hi" her mind went blank unless she was talking to Cindy. After all, what was there to talk about? No one would be interested in the biographies of famous mathematicians and scientists she had read over the summer.

She opened her top book, as usual, and started reading as she headed toward the physics room. It seemed as if there were never enough time in one day to do all the reading she wanted to.

No one else was in the classroom yet. She slid into a front seat again, then stacked all of her books on the shelf under her desk except the one which she was reading.

She was so engrossed in the life of Isaac Newton that she didn't realize someone else had entered the room and sat in the seat behind her.

"So, we meet again!" Bruce's voice sounded warm and friendly, but it surprised E.E. so much that she jumped like an idiot.

She turned around and smiled, but a "hi" was the

only word she could manage to squeak out. There was something about Bruce that really undid her.

Enviously, E.E. thought of Cindy and her carefree, easy way with boys. What a silly thing to think about! She didn't even want to have anything to do with boys, she reminded herself.

"Eureka! That's it," Bruce said, snapping his fingers.

"What's it?" E.E. asked, curious in spite of herself.

"Your name, of course! Eureka Estelle."

"It's Elizabeth Ellen," E.E. answered with a laugh.

"I like that much better than E.E. Mind if I call you Elizabeth?"

Shyly, E.E. lowered her eyes. She knew she couldn't trust her voice, so she merely shook her head in reply.

It was a relief when several other students walked in at that moment, followed by Mr. Creason, the physics teacher.

E.E. forgot about everything else when the class began. She listened intently as he gave them the same talk that most of the teachers gave at the beginning of the school year about what was expected of them, and so on.

"One other thing," Mr. Creason said at the conclusion of his talk. "In this class, an A means you have done an exceptional job. I only give A's if you do extra credit work."

There was a low murmur of protest from a few students who weren't already aware of Mr. Creason's manner of grading, but Elizabeth felt a warm sense of satisfaction. Who wanted to make an A without having to put forth any effort?

The remainder of the period was spent going over how their notebooks were to be kept, how to figure the percentage of error in their experiments, and the care of the apparatus they would be using.

As she listened to Mr. Creason teach, E.E. knew this would be one of her favorite classes. He challenged everyone to learn—to discover how, when, where, why. The anticipation of new knowledge gave her a familiar, heady feeling.

After Mr. Creason gave them an assignment and some time to work on it in class, the room grew silent except for the scratching of pencils against paper and the snapping of looseleaf notebooks opening and closing.

E.E. flipped open her *Modern Physics* book once more. She had turned to the exact page when they discussed the lesson. This time she opened the hardcover and happened to glance down. There in bold round letters was printed the name: BRUCE JOHNSON.

E.E. caught her bottom lip under her teeth. Of all the luck! She and Bruce must have inadvertently switched books after their crash. Now she would have to talk to him again, and that's exactly what she didn't want to do. She wanted to avoid Bruce Johnson as much as possible.

E.E. didn't realize she had been holding her breath until she let it out in a low sigh. If she could just finish the book transaction as quickly as possible when class was over, maybe it wouldn't be too bad. She suddenly felt so bungling and shy at the prospect of talking to Bruce about anything. What if she dropped another book?

Her hands grew moist and she wished desperately for the bell to ring. But when it did, she gathered up her belongings as slowly as possible while she practiced what she was going to say. At last, with Bruce's physics book ready, she turned to face him.

At the same moment, he turned around and started toward the door. She opened her mouth to call after him, then closed it again. He was already surrounded by a group of boys.

Oh, well, she thought with a slight shrug. She could always give it to him later. She hadn't wanted to talk to him, anyway, and it didn't matter to her if he went on his way without so much as a "Bye" or "See you later."

She didn't care at all. But still, a hard ball formed in the center of her stomach and seemed to grow larger and larger, pressing against her ribs until it was difficult to breathe.

2

"Hey, there you are," Cindy's cheery voice called.

"Hi," E.E. said, looking up from her book and smiling at the cute, bouncy, blond girl who was coming to meet her in the hall.

"What do you mean, *hi?*" Cindy demanded. "You were supposed to wait for me by the physics room so we could walk out to the bus together. Remember?"

"Oh, wow! I forgot all about it," E.E. said. "I'm really sorry."

"You'll make a great absentminded professor someday," Cindy said with a teasing tone. "Honestly though, E., if you don't quit walking around with your nose in a book, you're going to crash into someone one of these days!"

Though her heart quickened, E.E. kept a blank look on her face. "There is that possibility," she said in a grave tone.

Cindy waggled a finger at her in exasperation. "I'm being serious."

"So am I." That was the best way to be when she wanted to throw Cindy off track, E.E. had found out a long time ago.

"Sure you are. It would serve you right if you did collide with someone—preferably a boy."

"I guess we should hurry up," E.E. answered, hoping she could get Cindy's mind on something else. "We don't want to miss the bus."

"You're right," Cindy agreed.

They hurried to their lockers, which were just a short ways apart, and while Cindy began rummaging through hers, E.E. took out the rest of the books she wanted. By the time she finished, not one was left in her locker, and her friend was waiting with one book in her hand and a dismayed look on her face.

"Honestly," Cindy said, shaking her head slowly, "I don't think I'll ever get used to it."

"Used to what?" E.E. asked with a perplexed frown.

"You, of course. We've been neighbors since we were four, gone to school together from the time we were five—now here we are seniors and I still can't believe that you take every single book home every single night. And on the first day of school, no less!"

Laughing, E.E. handed part of the books to Cindy. "Here, if you carry some of them for me, maybe you'll believe it."

A group of girls approached them, laughing and chattering. They stopped at Marsha Thompson's locker and E.E. found herself listening to their conversation.

"Really, he's such a doll," Marsha said, rolling her big gray eyes. "With that sandy hair and freckles on his nose and those blue eyes . . ." Her voice trailed off, and Patty Benson continued.

"Mark says he's a fantastic football player. The coach is sure excited about having him on the team."

"Hi, Cindy," Tammi Smith called as Cindy and E.E. walked by. She nodded vaguely in E.E.'s direction. "They're talking about the new boy, Bruce Johnson," she explained. "Have you seen him yet?"

E.E. stood mutely, feeling strangely hot and cold at the same time as Cindy voiced her agreement that Bruce was indeed cute. Then Cindy and Tammi talked for a moment about their Wednesday cheerleading practice.

By the time the two girls reached the bus, there were only a couple of seats left at the front. The driver closed the door with a loud thump after they climbed aboard.

As they took their seat, Cindy resumed a one-sided conversation about Bruce. "That new boy really is good looking," she said with a dreamy look. "I've heard he's a nice guy, too—friendly with everyone. All the guys on the football team like him. I wouldn't mind dating him myself," she concluded, as she settled back into her seat.

"If you want to, then you probably will," E.E. said. "Everyone wants to go with a cheerleader, especially a cute one."

E.E. meant the words in all sincerity, and Cindy smiled her appreciation. "You haven't happened to notice Bruce, have you?" she asked.

The question surprised her, making E.E. feel unexpectedly flustered. She didn't want to lie and yet her encounter with Bruce was something she

didn't even feel like sharing with Cindy. "Well
. . . I . . . uh, yes," she stammered. "He is in a
couple of my classes."

Cindy narrowed her eyes and studied her thoughtfully, while she rubbed a temple slowly with her
forefinger. "There's more to it than that," she said at
last.

E.E. concentrated on using her blank look, but it
didn't faze Cindy.

"Come on, E.," she prodded. "Tell me the rest.
I'm dying of curiosity."

"It wasn't anything. We just kind of met outside
the library and he carried some of my books to trig
for me." E.E. ducked her head to hide her embarrassment.

"You're kidding!" Cindy said, with wide eyes.

"Would I kid?" E.E. asked in a light voice.

"That would be unusual," Cindy agreed. "And
you say it wasn't anything. Ha!"

In a short while, the bus reached their corner and
the girls got off to walk the two blocks home.

"You know, I've been thinking," Cindy began
slowly.

"Scheming is probably more the word you have in
mind," E.E. interrupted.

"There's no reason why you shouldn't be the girl
to date Bruce," Cindy continued in an excited voice.
"I could come over tonight. We could do something
to your hair and maybe put together a really neat
outfit for you to wear tomorrow. I could give you a
few lessons in——"

"No!" E.E. cried desperately. "A thousand times,

no. You ought to know by now you won't get me to go along with something like that."

"You can't blame me for trying," Cindy said as the Kirkpatricks' bulldog rushed up to the fence, barking furiously at them. "You're a neat person, but you won't give anyone a chance to find out. Now if you'd just——"

"Huh-uh," E.E. said, shaking her head. "Let's drop it, okay?"

"Only for the time being," Cindy answered as she turned in at her gate. "See you later."

The spicy smell of warm cinnamon rolls greeted Elizabeth when she stepped in the door of their small brick home a few moments later.

"I'm home, Mom," she called, heading for the kitchen.

Dorothy Clark was placing one of her freshly baked rolls on a dessert plate when E.E. came in and plopped her books on the kitchen table.

"Smells better than a bakery in here," E.E. said, sniffing appreciatively. Taking a glass from the cupboard, she went over to the refrigerator and poured herself a glass of milk.

Her mother poured a cup of coffee and sat down at the table with her.

"You're not having a roll with me?" E.E. asked.

"I'd better not," her mother said, patting her ample waist.

E.E. smiled across the table at her short, plump, gray-haired mother. She was always watching her weight one day and forgetting about it the next. If she wouldn't bake such delicious things all the time, maybe she wouldn't have such a hard time.

"Did you have a good day, honey?" her mother asked.

E.E. nodded, her mouth full of roll. They sat together in a comfortable silence while she finished her snack.

A warm sense of contentment enveloped E.E. This was one of her favorite places. The cheery kitchen with its red checkered curtains and matching table cloth on the Early American table always bolstered her spirits. And it was pleasant to come home every day to the smell of something freshly baked, knowing exactly where her mother would be.

E.E. stole a quick peek at her mother, now. She looks as if she could be my grandmother sitting there instead of my mom, E.E. thought with a shock. She easily could be. A lot of kids had fifty-eight-year-old grandmothers instead of fifty-eight-year-old mothers. But this was her own dear, old, sweet mom, who had found out at the age of forty-one that she was expecting her first baby. Talk about a shock. That must have really been one.

Picking up the brochure that was laying on the table, E.E. flipped through it. "I see Daddy's still looking at travel trailers."

"Yes," her mother answered, "and with all his great plans for traveling after he retires, I bet I won't get him any further than the lake."

"Maybe you will," E.E. said. Resisting the desire for another cinnamon roll, she carried her plate and glass over to the sink. She had managed to remain thin in spite of her mother's cooking, but she wouldn't if she ate too much. "What can I do to help you with supper?" she asked, rinsing out her glass.

"You can make the salad. Everything else is ready since we're having pot roast."

E.E. ran the lettuce under the water and began tearing it into bite-size pieces. "What you need, Mom, is about twelve kids to cook for instead of just Dad and me."

"I'd like that," her mother said with a far-away look in her eyes. Then she shook her head as if to clear it of such a silly notion. "But I was just blessed with one," she said, as she came over to get the dish cloth.

After transferring E.E.'s books to an empty space on the cabinet, she wiped the table and set it for supper.

When Elizabeth had finished with the salad, she took her books to her room to study for a while before her father came home and it was time to eat.

Sitting down at the small walnut desk her mother and she had refinished, E.E. let her eyes wander slowly over her room. It was neat, but she had never really done anything to decorate it. She was satisfied with the off-white walls, the plain blue ribcord spread that covered her bed, and the matching ribcord drapes at both windows. As long as she had plenty of bookshelves, which she did, that was all she cared about.

She pulled out Bruce's physics book to read the assignment for tomorrow, opened the front cover, and stared at the neat round letters once more. Without any intention of doing so, she traced over them with her finger. BRUCE JOHNSON—a nice name, but it made a funny feeling flutter through her, and she wasn't certain what the reason was.

Suddenly restless, she stood up and walked over to stand in front of the full-length mirror on her closet door. She already knew what she would see, so why bother to look?

There was nothing in her appearance that would attract a boy—long brown hair pulled back severely from her face, large hazel eyes behind horn-rimmed glasses giving her a slightly owlish appearance, and white even teeth. She was definitely a plain Jane, even dressing like one in her brown or gray skirts and her oxford-style blouses.

So why had Bruce treated her differently? Almost as if she were a really attractive girl? Maybe it was just her imagination, but she had felt certain at the time that there was a spark of something between them, at least for a moment.

Kicking off her loafers, she flopped back on her bed and stared up at the ceiling. Why was she having such ridiculous thoughts? The situation was utterly hopeless, and besides that, she'd made herself a promise. Forcing everything else from her mind, she returned to her desk and began studying with a vengeance.

3

During French class the following morning, Elizabeth received a message to report to Mrs. Brice, the guidance counselor, during activity period.

Probably something to do with choosing a college, she thought, as she worked on a translation of "Sous Peine de Mort."

Two hours later as she sat in the chair facing Mrs. Brice's desk, she decided she must have been summoned on a different matter.

The middle-aged woman studied her with her brow furrowed in thought, and E.E. noticed that her light blue eyes didn't twinkle with their usual merriment.

"I've been going over your record, Elizabeth," she began slowly.

E.E. twisted uncomfortably in her chair and picked at an invisible speck on her skirt. Something was up; she could tell from the tone of Mrs. Brice's voice.

"Your grades couldn't be better, of course, but you haven't been involved in any activities in the last two years. I blame myself for letting this happen. I should have pushed you harder in the past."

She should have guessed what the guidance counselor had wanted to talk to her about today. E.E. squirmed again, but didn't say anything. Mrs. Brice had mentioned this same thing every semester for the last two years, and E.E. always promised to think about joining some extracurricular activity.

With approximately 600 students to keep tabs on, Mrs. Brice couldn't keep too close a watch over her, and after E.E.'s promise, the subject was usually dropped until the next semester.

"I know what you're thinking," Mrs. Brice said, "but you're not wiggling out of it this year. I'm going to insist that you have an activity to round out your otherwise excellent record for college. I think some type of social service would be best for you." Mrs. Brice gazed at her steadily, obviously waiting for an answer.

"I'll think about it," E.E. murmured, "and——"

"Not this time." The silver-blond-haired woman shook her head and tapped her nails on the desk top. "I've already found the perfect thing."

Elizabeth felt trapped, as if the four walls of the office were closing in on her. There was no law which stated a person had to join an extracurricular activity, she thought sullenly.

She would listen first, but there was no reason she couldn't refuse to go along with Mrs. Brice's great idea. Swallowing hard at the lump in her throat, she waited for the guidance counselor to continue.

"The grade school needs volunteers to help with its Learning Disability classes. We've already arranged for some of our students to help three days a week during activity period."

Elizabeth stared at her in disbelief. "Y-you want me to do something like that?" Her voice sounded strained and she could feel every muscle in her body growing tense.

"That's exactly what I want you to do," Mrs. Brice stated firmly.

"What would it involve?" E.E. asked. Her throat felt uncommonly dry.

"Mostly tutoring on a one-to-one basis, though I don't know the exact responsibilities."

"B-but," E.E. stammered, raising her hands in a helpless gesture, then letting them fall to her lap, "I wouldn't have any idea what to do!"

"Try, Elizabeth, and you might surprise yourself. You have such a vast amount of potential, if you would only let someone or something crack that protective shell of yours."

The guidance counselor's last statement made E.E. feel suddenly conspicuous as if she were overhearing a conversation about herself. Sometimes Mrs. Brice reminded her of Cindy, the way she tried to push and prod her. She could feel her heart hammering against her ribs, and wished somehow that she could get out of this without disappointing Mrs. Brice.

"What do you say?" Mrs. Brice asked. "The program starts next week. Can I put your name down?"

"N-not yet. Can't I have at least one day to think about it?" E.E. pleaded.

Mrs. Brice nodded. "I'll set up another appointment with you for the same time tomorrow. Talk it over with your parents tonight; I'm certain they'll agree that it's a good idea."

Elizabeth left the guidance office feeling discouraged and disgusted at the same time. It wasn't fair for people to try and run her life. Why couldn't everyone just leave her alone?

E.E. glanced down at the watch circling her small wrist. She usually spent activity period in the library and she still had quite a bit of time left.

Even though Mrs. Brice had encouraged her to talk to her parents, E.E. knew she wouldn't. They would think whatever she decided was the right thing, anyway. Her folks were good people and sweet, but they allowed her to have her own way most of the time. She heaved her shoulders and sighed.

"It can't be that bad," a cheerful voice called.

She looked up to see Bruce standing by his locker. Part of her wanted to be friendly and the other part wanted to run and hide.

Her tongue felt as if it were stuck to the roof of her mouth as she answered him. "I suppose you're right." She paused, trying to think of something friendly to say. "So, how do you like school so far?" she asked at last.

"Fine. Wait a minute and I'll walk with you." He grabbed his notebook off the top shelf and slammed the locker door with a clang. "Where are you headed, anyway?"

"The library."

"Me, too. Which one of the clubs are you joining?"

he asked as he swung along beside her in an easy manner.

"Oh . . . uh . . . what do you mean?" E.E. questioned, feeling foolish. The meeting with Mrs. Brice still occupied her thoughts, and now she wondered if she had missed out on part of what Bruce had said.

"You know—the Great Books and Math clubs are both having their organizational meetings in the library in exactly five minutes. With everything else I have to do, I'll only have time for one club, and I still haven't decided which one it will be. Which one of those do you think is best?"

She swallowed hard. Bruce was actually looking at her as if he valued her opinion. It was necessary for her to say something.

"Well, actually," she said, stopping to clear her throat, "I guess they're both fine."

"Well, which one are you joining?"

Here was the answer to her dilemma! When she met with Mrs. Brice tomorrow, she could tell her that she had decided to join a club instead of helping at the grade school. Math Club only met once a month. Surely she could stand attending nine times during the school year. If not, she could skip a few meetings. "Math club," she answered decisively.

"Then that's good enough for me, too," Bruce said, smiling down at her.

A miserable feeling welled up in her. It was hypocritical to make Bruce think she was something that she wasn't, but it was the perfect solution to her problem.

When she and Bruce walked into the library together a few minutes later, everyone looked up in surprise. They walked over to the corner where the Math Club was meeting, and the president, Dan Wright, welcomed them both. He then proceeded to describe the various activities of the club for all of the prospective members.

When activity period ended, Bruce turned to E.E. "You were right. This does seem like a good club. Shall we go pay our dues?"

E.E. nodded shyly.

"What's your next class?" Bruce asked when they were finished.

"History."

"I have German. See you later," he said as he left.

E.E. was glad that she and Bruce had to head in opposite directions. She liked him and his attention, but it scared her. Did he really like her or was he just being friendly? Somehow she didn't want to find out. She didn't even want to think about him. So why did she keep doing *exactly* that?

She asked herself the same question that evening when she took out her physics book to read. It wasn't her book. She had forgotten to exchange with Bruce, and just the knowledge that she held his book in her hands made his image flash before her—friendly blue eyes, broad shoulders, athletic build.

She didn't know much about football, but he did look as if he would be a good player. She could picture his large rawboned hands gripping the football as he loped down the field for a touchdown.

Shaking her head, she mentally berated herself for letting thoughts of Bruce interrupt her studying.

There was a light tap on the door, and she glanced up to see her mother standing there.

"Come out to the living room for a little while, dear," she said. "Your father and I want to talk to you."

Her mom looked so serious with the vertical frown lines on her forehead. Had something terrible happened? E.E. could feel the blood draining from her face as her heart gave a lurch. Maybe something was wrong with one of her parents and they had been keeping it from her. She couldn't bear it if anything happened to her mom or dad.

"Don't look so alarmed, honey," Dorothy said, waiting for her in the hall.

There was the barest whisper of sound as Elizabeth let out a breath of relief before she stood up and went to join her parents in the living room.

Her father was sitting in his reclining chair watching a football game when she and Dorothy walked in. He righted the chair and clicked off the television.

It had to be something serious, E.E. thought, if her dad were willing to miss out on part of a football game.

"Sit down, hon," Herb Clark said, nodding toward the closest end of the sofa as he peered over his spectacles at her.

Elizabeth sat down slowly, imagining all kinds of terrible things. Maybe one of her parents had cancer, or what if her father had found out he had heart trouble when he went for his last checkup? It was all her fault . . . she should have been helping them more. After all, they weren't getting any younger.

She glanced from her dad's face, lined with smile

wrinkles at the corners of his brown eyes, to her mother's round one, usually so cheerful and now so worried looking. She could have been mowing the grass for her dad and insisting on doing the housework for her mom.

"Mrs. Brice called and talked to your mother today," her father began.

Elizabeth felt so relieved when he mentioned Mrs. Brice that at first she could feel nothing else. Then, slowly, a kind of righteous indignation took over as he continued to talk.

"Your mother and I agree that it would be a good idea for you to help with this program at the grade school," he concluded, setting his mouth in a determined line.

"But, Daddy," E.E. protested. "I joined Math Club today. Surely that's enough." She looked quickly at her mother for support.

"That's wonderful, Elizabeth," her mom said with enthusiasm. "There's no reason why you can't be in both."

"I don't think either of you understand," E.E. said. "I really don't want to do either."

"I was looking at your yearbooks from the last two years," her father said, making no comment on Elizabeth's last statement. "Both of the valedictorians and salutatorians were leaders in the school and belonged to every club imaginable. You will probably be valedictorian this year, and you've never been in one extracurricular activity."

"Why should I have to be like everyone else?" E.E. asked quietly.

"Maybe she's right, Herb," her mother said. "We're not trying to pour her into a mold."

"No, Dottie," her dad answered, and E.E. was surprised at the authoritative tone in his voice. He didn't sound at all like the mild-mannered father she was used to.

"You've always been a good daughter, and maybe that's part of the problem. We've protected and coddled you, and let you have your own way. But there's a real world out there, honey, and it's going to be our fault if you're not ready to face it."

"It's not fair for you to make me do something without even listening to my side," E.E. said.

"Why are you so opposed to helping someone else?" her father asked sternly.

His change of tactics threw her completely off guard. "Because . . . I . . ." E.E. stumbled over the words, searching her mind for a convincing argument, but she couldn't think of a thing that wouldn't sound selfish and conceited.

She could tell from the tone of her father's voice that she would have to have an awfully good reason, indeed. "I . . . don't know," she finished lamely, slumping back into the sofa.

4

"I couldn't stay out of this kitchen any longer," Herb Clark said, walking in the next evening as E.E. and Cindy pulled the last sheet of chocolate chip cookies out of the oven.

"Now, Daddy," E.E. warned. "Don't you get into them. Cindy bought all the stuff herself and the cookies are for the cheerleaders' bake sale."

"Help yourself, Mr. Clark," Cindy said. "After all, you're the one paying the gas bill for the oven I used."

"Thanks, Cindy," he said, taking several. "I knew I could count of you."

"It's positively depressing," Dorothy said. She was standing in the kitchen doorway shaking her head slowly.

"What's depressing, Mom?" E.E. asked, genuinely concerned. "Is something wrong?"

"Yes. It's not fair that you three can gobble down everything in sight and not gain an ounce, and I've probably put on ten pounds just from the smell drifting into the living room."

Everyone laughed, but E.E. couldn't help feeling a little sorry for her mother. Although she and her dad, and Cindy, too, were all the perfect weight, her mother definitely was on the "pleasingly plump" side.

Herb patted Dorothy's cheek and they walked back into the living room together. Then E.E. and Cindy grabbed a couple of cookies apiece, and went to E.E.'s room.

"It's hard to believe we're finally seniors," Cindy said, as she sat down in the cricket rocker in the corner of E.E.'s room.

"I know," E.E. agreed, sitting cross-legged on the floor and leaning back against her bed. "Too bad we didn't get any classes together besides English Lit."

"That would be hard to do when you take things like trigonometry and physics. You *could* join some of the clubs I'm in, though."

"Don't have time," E.E. said between bites of cookie. "Not since I'm in those other two things."

"You haven't told me anything about Math Club and this Learning Disability thing. I can't believe you finally decided to join something."

"There's nothing to tell yet," E.E. answered. "I don't know anything about either one." She didn't add that she hadn't really had a choice in the matter.

"Well, at least tell me why you got involved," Cindy said. "It's not like you at all, you've got to admit. The next thing I know you'll be running for Year Book Queen or going to the Harvest Ball with the captain of the football team."

"Good grief, I hope not," E.E. said. "Dana Stevens might not appreciate my dating her steady."

"Well, maybe you could go to the ball with a regular football player," Cindy continued. "For instance . . . oh, how about Bruce Johnson?"

E.E. stuffed the last bite of cookie into her mouth and purposely mumbled an incoherent reply, but Cindy wasn't going to be sidetracked.

"How are you and he getting along, anyway?" she asked, regarding E.E. with large expressive eyes.

E,E. shrugged noncommittally, but she felt as if an emotional tug-of-war were being played inside her. "I don't intend to have anything to do with any boy!" she blurted at last, surprising even herself with the vehemence of her words. Her short outburst made her feel almost weak, and left a strangely bitter taste in her mouth.

"Because of Tom," Cindy said softly. "You ought to realize what a ridiculous reason that is. I don't think you even liked him that much. But you do like Bruce, don't you?" she demanded.

Elizabeth nodded slowly. "B-but you don't understand. Something in me just kind of freezes up when I think about having a boyfriend." She sat there staring into space, twisting a strand of hair around her finger. She'd like to discuss the whole thing with Cindy, but what could she say when she didn't even understand her own feelings?

"Oh, for goodness sake," Cindy exclaimed in exasperation. "Just because one dumb boy takes you out a few times and drops you. Do you think you're the only girl that's ever happened to?"

"No, and I suppose I didn't like him that much.

But it was so humiliating," E.E. said. "What if Bruce is the same way?"

"What if he *isn't?* You could at least give yourself a chance to find out."

"I don't know," E.E. said, leaning her head back against the bed and closing her eyes. "You make it sound so easy, but it's not for me. I don't know how to act around a boy, and even when I want to be friendly, I find myself withdrawing."

Feeling terribly embarrassed at baring her thoughts even to Cindy, E.E. hopped to her feet and quickly changed the subject. "We'd better get out to the kitchen and box those cookies while there's still some left. You never know how many Daddy might eat if we leave them unprotected too long. There's the book you wanted to borrow," she said, waving her hand toward her desk.

"I do have to get home and study," Cindy said, standing, "but that wasn't too subtle."

Later that night, when she had gone to bed, E.E. thought about her conversation with Cindy. Sometimes Cindy acted as if she knew more about her than E.E. knew about herself.

But she didn't, E.E. thought as she pulled the covers up under her chin and snuggled into the pillow. After all, Cindy had never had trouble making friends. Everyone liked her. She had no idea what it was like to be on the outside looking in.

It was a strange kind of loneliness, as if she were watching the world from behind a two-way mirror. Cindy seemed to think that there was some kind of magic switch E.E. could flip on if only she wanted to, and zap! her whole personality would change.

Rolling onto her stomach, Elizabeth gave her pillow a savage punch. The total darkness of the room as she reached over and clicked off her lamp seemed to be an exact picture of the way she felt: drifting around in a black void with no one who really understood her.

Wasn't it enough that she had joined Math Club and finally agreed to help with the class at the grade school? Everyone seemed to be on her case—Mrs. Brice, her parents, and now Cindy pestering her about Bruce.

But Cindy *was* right about him. She did like Bruce—a whole lot. Why? why? why? she thought, hitting her pillow again. But then again, why not? Maybe she should just relax and let things work out on their own.

It was strange the next day that she and Bruce almost ran into each other again at exactly the same time and place as they had on the first day of school.

When E.E. walked out the library door and found herself face to face with him, something in her heart did a little skip. As their eyes met and he smiled that slow, crooked smile of his, she could feel the skip changing into a leap.

"Going my way?" he asked.

"Maybe," E.E. responded with an answering smile, as a strange tingling pulsed through her veins.

Bruce turned and they started walking in the direction of the math room.

"I seemed to have picked up your physics book by mistake the other day," he said, pulling it out from under his trig book.

"Oh, that's right," E.E. answered lightly. Thank goodness that was taken care of so easily.

After they switched books, Bruce began talking about the first football game coming up that Friday evening. E.E. was surprised how at ease she felt, walking down the hall with Bruce and listening to him talk.

"Do you like football?" he asked when they arrived at the classroom.

"Well . . . I really don't know much about it," she admitted.

If he was interested in me at all, he won't be now, she thought dejectedly.

"It's fun, but there's more important things in life, for sure," Bruce said.

She was glad that she had been honest with him. He didn't seem to mind at all.

Bruce was nice the rest of the week, always waving if he saw her in the hall, and speaking to her in trig and physics. He even walked with her from one class to the other a couple of times. But she couldn't be sure yet that he really liked her. After all, she saw him talking to other girls, too, and lots of guys.

Bruce is just an outgoing person who makes friends easily, she told herself. He doesn't like me any more than he does anyone else. I musn't get my hopes up.

On Friday, Bruce was waiting for her when she came out of the library.

"Hi," he greeted her. "I was hoping I'd find you here."

"What can I do for you?" E.E. asked in a teasing way.

"As a matter of fact, there is something," Bruce said as they walked along.

E.E.'s heart seemed to stand still. Maybe he would ask her for a date. She knew she would say yes, but suddenly she felt so drab and blah in comparison to this tall, muscular, handsome boy walking beside her. If he really did ask her out, she would have to ask Cindy for a few pointers.

"I was wondering if you'd like to go to the library with me tomorrow afternoon and study for that physics test coming up? We could get a Coke afterward at the drugstore." He stopped and looked down at her, waiting for an answer.

E.E. felt rooted to the spot. Her heart seemed to freeze to a stop this time, as all the memories of last spring came rushing back. What if Bruce were just like Tom? If only there were some way to find out for sure before she answered him.

Taking a deep breath, she spoke in a shaky voice. "I'll have to check on family plans first." She didn't sound very convincing, but it was the best way she could think of to stall for time.

"Fine," Bruce answered. "I can give you a call this evening."

E.E. questioned Bruce's motives as she sat through trig. Maybe he was like Tom and needed help with his homework so he could remain eligible for football. What if that was the only reason he seemed interested in her? She couldn't stand to go through that again. And yet it could just be coincidental that he asked her for the same kind of date Tom had always taken her on.

When trig was over, E.E. remembered she had left

her physics paper in her locker, so she hurried back to get it. Though she never intentionally listened to other people's conversations, she couldn't help doing so today. Even amid the clanking of locker doors and the shuffling of feet, she could hear the two girls' words from where they stood at Marsha Thompson's locker.

"As far as I know," Marsha was saying, "you're the first girl Bruce has asked out since he's been at dear old Falls City High. But what's Dave going to say?"

"He'd better not say anything," Tammi Smith said with a laugh. "After all, we're not going steady."

"Where's he taking you?"

"To a movie, then some place for a hamburger. I can hardly wait for Saturday night. I hope he's as neat as I think he is!"

E.E. slammed her locker door and hurried past the two girls in the hall. She was almost trembling from the words she'd overheard. She had her answer—Bruce didn't like her at all. He only needed help studying for his physics test.

What other proof did she need? He planned to take Tammi to a movie and probably the Snuggle In afterward, and he had asked E.E. to go to the library and the corner drugstore for a coke. Undoubtedly he hoped no one would see them together if they went to the drugstore!

A carousel of emotions began to whirl inside her to a tune of self-loathing: anger, disgust, hurt, embarrassment.

She rushed into the girls' restroom, thankful to see that no one was there as hot, angry tears began to blur her vision. How could she have been so dumb?

E.E. splashed some cool water on her face, then taking a deep breath, she straightened her shoulders and marched back out the door. Bruce Johnson wouldn't have another chance to try and make a fool of her. She would tell him after class that she had no intention of going anywhere with him. And after that she wasn't going to have another thing to do with him!

5

Elizabeth awoke Monday morning with her mother shaking her by the shoulder.

"Wake up, dear," she said. "You've overslept and you're going to be late if you don't hurry."

As her mother left the room, E.E. padded across the carpeted floor to her small bathroom, where she brushed her teeth and washed her face. The solemn eyes staring back at her from the mirror seemed to verify her sentiments that it was going to be a lousy day. She was already off to a late start.

After brushing her shining chestnut hair, she fastened it back out of her way and went to the closet to find something to wear. She put on the first skirt and blouse she found, then pulled on a pair of hose.

She had just finished getting ready when her mother called to say that Cindy was waiting. With a backward glance at her unmade bed, she gathered her belongings and rushed out to the kitchen.

"Bye, Mom," she said, as she took the piece of

toast her mother handed her and went out the door with Cindy.

"I can't believe you actually overslept," Cindy said as they headed for the bus stop. "You do look a bit rumpled, though, as if you got ready in a hurry," she added in a teasing voice.

"Thanks a lot, friend," E.E. retorted, but she had to grin.

"Seriously, though," Cindy said. "You look so nice with your contacts for a change. Why don't you start wearing them all the time?"

E.E. stopped short and let out a moan. "I don't have my contacts in, I forgot my glasses. I'll have to go back."

"There's the bus," Cindy said, pointing across the vacant lot to the opposite corner.

"Mom will have to bring us."

"That's okay. I'd better go on. We've got to practice some cheers and there's just enough time to get to the bus. See you later," Cindy said as they headed in opposite directions.

She was lucky this wasn't Dad's week to drive, E.E. thought as she walked back to the house. Even so, her mother didn't like to drive and wouldn't be too happy about taking her.

Her mom was still in the kitchen and insisted on E.E.'s eating something more substantial before she took her to school.

After eating, E.E. went in to get her glasses and decided to make her bed as long as she had time. Hopefully the rest of the day would be better, she thought, as she tossed her pillow into the rocking chair and began pulling up the sheet and smoothing it.

It probably wouldn't, though. This was D-Day, when they went to the grade school for the first time to help with the Learning Disability program. No telling how that would go, but she wasn't anxious to find out.

She hated any kind of change, she had to admit. Give her a nice familiar rut and she was content. It seemed as if everything were destined to change, though, regardless of whether she wanted it to or not.

By the time E.E. finished with her bed, her mother already had the Ford backed out of the garage and was waiting for her. As she climbed in the car, she leaned back, closed her eyes, and let out a long sigh.

"Are you all right, dear?" her mother asked. "It's not like you to oversleep."

"I'm fine," E.E. murmured. "I just haven't slept too well the last few nights."

"I know you're worried about helping with that class today, but don't look so glum. It will be all right, you'll see." Reaching over, she gave Elizabeth's hand a squeeze.

"It's okay," E.E. answered, shrugging her shoulders. She didn't intend to tell her mother that was only half of what was bothering her. Thinking about Bruce had kept her awake for the last few nights.

"Do you know what I think would be good for you?" her mother asked as she backed the car out of the driveway and headed north on Monroe Street.

"What's that?" E.E. asked without too much interest. Knowing her mom, she would probably suggest making a cheesecake for dinner since that was E.E.'s favorite dessert. She always thought the way to cheer someone up was through their stomach.

"What you need is a change," her mom said. "Why don't you take Cindy shopping with you? She could help you pick out a couple of pretty outfits. If you want, you can get an appointment to have your hair cut and styled. You can even decorate your room if you'd like to," she went on enthusiastically.

Elizabeth felt as if her smile were changing into a grimace. Why was everyone, including her own mother, trying to make her into something she wasn't? No one ever seemed to be dissatisfied with her before. Why did they suddenly find her so repulsive?

"Thanks, Mom, but I don't think so," she said, shaking her head slowly.

They drove the rest of the way in silence. When her mother left her off at the corner by the high school, E.E. forced a grin on her face and a cheery note to her voice as she told her mother good-bye. There was no reason to leave her mom feeling miserable just because that was the way she felt.

Activity period arrived much too quickly as far as E.E. was concerned. She would rather prolong her suffering than get it over with. She was still trying to think of any possible excuse to get out of helping as she walked to guidance office where the six volunteers were supposed to meet.

Rita Mitchell, Sheryl Lawrence, and David McGraw, all seniors, were already in the room talking with Mrs. Brice.

"Hello, Elizabeth," Mrs. Brice greeted her, then looked up at the clock on the wall. "As soon as our two other fellows arrive, we can be on our way. Ordinarily you'll walk the three blocks to Washington School, but I'm driving everyone over this time."

She had just finished speaking when the office door opened, and Paul Reynolds walked in followed by Bruce Johnson.

E.E. felt a little quiver which seemed to start in the center of her stomach and spread out in little waves throughout her body. She ducked her head and didn't look at Bruce. If only she had known that he was one of the people in on this, she would have gotten out of it some way!

"We're taking the school's station wagon that's parked in the east lot," Mrs. Brice told them. "I'll lock up and meet you there."

Though the boys waited for the girls to go out first, they soon by-passed them in the hall. E.E. felt as if she were a third bookend as she walked along with Rita and Sheryl. The two were old friends, and were busy chattering about something.

E.E.'s steps lagged and in a short time she was walking alone down the almost deserted halls. Then she heard the click, click of high heels and soon Mrs. Brice was walking beside her.

"Why so dismal looking, Elizabeth?" Mrs. Brice asked, looking at her with obvious concern. "I know you feel as if you've been drafted, but sometimes draftees make the best soldiers. You'll do great."

E.E. nodded, but she didn't trust herself to speak. If everyone was so solicitous of her feelings, why did they keep shoving her into unwelcome situations?

She felt as if she'd been thrown into a gigantic pressure pot.

As they walked down the sidewalk and across the paved parking area, E.E. discovered to her dismay that the two girls were already seated in the front seat of the station wagon. There was a school rule that no more than three could ride in front, so that left her to scrunch in back with the boys.

Bruce pushed open the back door for her. She was going to have to sit by him! The realization made her bones feel as if they had turned to jelly. Why was it when you decided not to have anything to do with someone, they turned up everywhere? she wondered. Thank goodness they were only riding to school this one time.

Lifting her chin and gritting her teeth, she slid into the small space beside him and slammed the door. She felt horribly conscious of his arm and leg pressing against hers and she could feel her muscles growing tense, but there was nowhere to move.

As Bruce mumbled a "Hi" then started talking to the boy on the other side of him, E.E. felt relief mingled at the same time with melancholy. She had let him know that she didn't care to go out with him last Thursday after physics. It would have been wonderful if he had been different, but she was lucky she had found out as soon as she did. Ever since then, she had completely ignored him.

The three-block drive to the grade school seemed more like three miles. Elizabeth was careful not to glance at Bruce any of that time, but studiously looked out the window at the bright, sunshiny day.

As soon as Mrs. Brice parked, E.E. was the first to hop out of the car.

Washington School was a new, single-story, green block building similar in construction to the other two grade schools in Falls City. E.E. had a fleeting wish that Lincoln School was where they would be helping, the one she and Cindy had attended from kindergarten through the sixth grade. At least she would be more familiar with the territory. It was a silly notion, though. Something like that wouldn't help at all.

Mrs. Brice led the way to a room where six chairs were arranged in a semicircle around a desk, and a woman who introduced herself as a Miss Kirkpatrick was waiting to talk to them. Their guidance counselor sat down in another seat by the door.

For some reason, E.E. had been expecting the L.D. teacher to be old and crochety, but Miss Kirkpatrick was in about her late twenties with shoulder-length copper-colored hair and a svelte figure.

She began to talk to them in a pleasant voice, punctuating her words with a smile. "First of all," she said, "I'd like to thank each one of you for volunteering to assist with our Learning Disability Program.

"I don't know if you know anything about Learning Disabilities, but they have nothing to do with intelligence. Hans Christian Anderson, Thomas Edison, President Wilson, and Nelson Rockefeller all had Learning Disabilities.

"These kids are smart, but it's as if they have a short circuit in certain areas of their brain. Some of them who have no problem with reading, have a terrible time with numbers. Others, who can do arithmetic, have trouble with reading. Some have a hard time with both. Sometimes a Learning Disability is not as severe as we think from looking at a child's work. Once they're motivated, many of them start overcoming their problem.

"Briefly, what we plan to do is assign each of you to a student who is doing poorly in the subject which you excel in."

Glancing at the notes in her hand, she read, "E.E. Clark, you will be helping Lisa Forrester with arithmetic."

She continued through the list. The others would be helping kids with reading and writing. Bruce was the only other person helping someone with math.

According to what Miss Kirkpatrick had just said, Bruce must be excellent in mathematics. That didn't mean he was smart in everything, though. Evidently he wasn't so great in physics if he wanted E.E. to help him study for the test this coming Friday.

Why was she thinking about Bruce again? E.E. wondered in disgust. She had already made it perfectly clear to him that she didn't want any more to do with him, and there was no doubt in her mind that he had received her message loud and clear. She shook her head slightly as if to rid herself of any more thoughts about Bruce Johnson.

6

After Miss Kirkpatrick explained to them exactly how the program operated, the smile on her face was replaced by a serious look.

"Before you meet the student you will be working with, I want to remind you—these are intelligent children. They will know right away if you are sincere. In order to expect any results from the efforts you put forth, you must be willing to involve yourself totally with the child you're helping. That means forgetting about yourself and your problems for a time and concentrating all your energies on another person.

"I already feel that you're a special group of guys and gals," she said with the smile back on her face. "It's not everyone who is willing to give part of themselves in this way to help another person."

E.E. squirmed uncomfortably and examined her clear, glossy nails. All this talk about involvement and giving yourself made her uneasy. It was exactly what she had decided to shy away from this year: becoming involved with anyone.

Besides that, she didn't know the first thing about children. Why, she'd never even babysat! What had Mrs. Brice gotten her into, anyway? A panicky feeling rose inside her as she waited for the teacher to finish her talk.

"All you'll have time for today is to meet the student you'll be working with." She handed a mimeographed sheet of paper to each of them. "Please read these before you come on Wednesday. Are there any questions?"

She waited a while and when no one said anything, she laughed and continued, "I'm glad I was so thorough, but feel free to talk to me any time a question does arise. Now, let's go meet your charges."

The panicky feeling began to grow until E.E. felt as if she were facing a volcano that was threatening to erupt.

She had so many qualms about what was happening. What if this little girl she was supposed to work with was a real brat? Miss Kirkpatrick said they should get involved, but how did she even do something like that?

She was still asking herself questions as they followed the two women into another room where six children of various age levels were sitting at two tables, working at different things.

Elizabeth's eyes wandered over the group, trying to pick out the girl who could be Lisa Forrester. She didn't have time to make her choice before Miss Kirkpatrick called Lisa over. She was a pretty little girl with short, dark brown hair the color of E.E.'s walnut desk and large brown eyes.

"Lisa is seven years old and in the second grade," Miss Kirkpatrick said after she introduced the two girls. "You two can get acquainted for a while," she said.

What am I supposed to do? E.E. wondered in consternation.

"Come on," Lisa said, grabbing her hand and leading the way to the table where she had been sitting. "How come Miss Kirkpatrick called you E.E.?" Lisa asked after they sat down. Her large eyes were round and questioning.

"That's what I said I wanted to be called."

"Don't you have a name?"

"It's Elizabeth, but my friends call me E.E."

"Oh." Lisa looked solemn and thoughtful for a moment before she flashed Elizabeth a big smile which revealed two dimples. "Then I guess that's what I'll have to call you because I want to be your friend, too."

E.E. could feel herself relaxing. There was something endearing about this pixie-faced seven-year-old. "I'm glad you feel that way, Lisa," she answered "Now tell me something about you. Do you have any brothers or sisters?"

"Two brothers," Lisa said, her face lighting up. "Jeff's in fourth grade and Brett's in sixth. How many do you have?"

"I don't have any." Were all children this easy to talk to? E.E. wondered. So far it wasn't anything like the frightening experience she had anticipated.

"That's awful," Lisa said, placing her elbow on the

table and propping her chin on her hand. "I'd like to have a sister, but at least I've got brothers. You don't have anybody."

E.E. couldn't help laughing at Lisa's seriousness. "I don't know that it's that bad."

In a few minutes it was time to leave, and Mrs. Brice drove everyone back to the high school. This time E.E. was the first one to scoot into the front seat, leaving one of the other girls to climb in back with the boys.

Somehow, the thought of helping Lisa with her arithmetic on Wednesday brightened the remainder of E.E.'s day. Maybe this experiment wouldn't turn out so badly after all, especially if she didn't have to sit by Bruce again.

That evening after dinner, she stretched across her bed and studied the paper Miss Kirkpatrick had given her, trying to imagine what it would be like when she actually started working with Lisa.

A brief analysis of Lisa's problem was written down and also a description of what Elizabeth was supposed to do in the thirty minutes of the coming Wednesday and Friday. She would administer a short test first, and all that was written down for the remainder of the time was:

"Help the student closely observe the shape, size, and color of objects in the classroom:

Round like the clock
Square like the bulletin board
Long like a pencil
Green like the walls
Small like the thumbtack

Have Lisa look around the room and find numbers. Ask her to locate a "1," etc. How many times can she find this number in the room?"

Elizabeth shook her head in puzzlement. This certainly sounded easy enough. Why would the school need anyone to help with something like that? It sounded more like thirty minutes of nursery school so the regular teachers could have a rest.

Oh, well, she thought, pursing her lips and rolling over to sit up. If this was all it was going to take to make everyone happy with her, she ought to be thankful that it was so easy. Besides that, she liked Lisa a lot, which completely surprised her since she'd never even noticed children before.

"Why all the facial contortions?" Cindy asked, walking into the room.

"Hi," E.E. said. "Didn't know you were standing there."

"The reason I came over was to talk about this huge paper Mrs. Whitman wants us to write for first semester. I want to get started on it right away. It could be too easy to put off."

"I'm still trying to decide exactly what I want to write about," E.E. said.

"I thought you were going to write about the similarities between the lives of Isaac Newton and Albert Einstein."

"I still might, but I haven't decided for sure."

"If you change your mind, let me know. Maybe I could write about that and impress Mrs. Whitman with my genius so I can make an A."

"Go ahead, if you want to. Somehow the idea doesn't really appeal to me any more."

"How did everything go today?" Cindy asked. "You never did say what you were making all those faces about when I came in."

"I was just looking at this," E.E. answered, waving the paper in her hand. "Take a look," she said, handing it to Cindy.

Cindy took the paper from her outstretched hand and settled down on a cushion on the floor. After studying it for a few moments, she looked up at E.E. "*This* is what you've been in such a state over the last few days? Sounds simple to me."

"I know, that's what puzzles me. It doesn't sound as if they really need our help at all."

"It might be harder than it seems," Cindy said in a serious voice. "After all, what do either of us know about Learning Disabilities?"

"Not much," E.E. said. "All I know is what Miss Kirkpatrick told us today. Still, I was expecting it to be really complicated, and I'm relieved it's not."

"It just proves my theory that you get too shook up about things that aren't that earth-shaking," Cindy teased.

E.E. sighed and rolled her eyes back. "And now for lecture number two thousand nine hundred seventy five, brought to us by Cindy Morris," she said, sounding like a tape recording.

"Would I lecture?" Cindy asked, trying to puff up indignantly. Instead she ended up laughing.

"Of course not," E.E. said blandly. "Whatever gave you that idea?"

"Now prying is another matter," Cindy went on. "I heard a neat bit of info today. Maybe you can tell me if it's true."

"What's that?"

"Only that Bruce Johnson was one of the six people chosen to help with the project you're on."

E.E.'s yes got caught in her throat so she nodded her head.

"You two may get together yet," Cindy said.

A sense of desolate frustration crept into E.E.'s chest and settled coldly in her heart. "I don't . . . think so," she said, the words almost a whisper.

"I don't understand what you've got against the guy. He's sharp, good-looking, a super football player——"

"He also asked me out for last Saturday afternoon," E.E. said with a bitter tone to her voice, "to study at the library for a physics test and get a Coke at the drugstore."

"O-o-o-o, that is bad," Cindy said, chewing thoughtfully on her bottom lip. "But he didn't know about . . . what I mean is, I'm sure it really upset you, but he might have thought you would really enjoy something like that. He seems like a very sincere person. It could have been a coincidence."

"I considered that possibility," E.E. answered through tight jaws, "until I heard that he had asked Tammi Smith to go to a movie the same evening. I might as well face it—no boy wants anything to do with me unless they need help studying. I guess my first instinct about him was right. He's someone I'll be better off staying away from."

"It doesn't sound too promising," Cindy agreed, "but somehow it doesn't seem to fit with his personality."

"Whether it does or not," E.E. answered, shrug

ging her shoulders, "I don't really want to think about it."

So why did she keep doing just that? she asked herself after Cindy left. Bruce seemed to be around every corner she turned. If she wasn't crashing into him, she was having to sit beside him. She was fortunate she had found out what he was really like.

Crossing the room to stand at her window, E.E. pulled back the curtain and peered out. A full moon hung in the sky, pouring its liquid gold over the landscape, but still there was a loneliness in the scene which matched her forlorn feelings.

A lump rose into her throat and a hollow ache squeezed around her heart. Was this sense of being alone and unwanted except by her family and Cindy going to continue forever?

There was love and laughter for others her age—why not for her? It was hard to admit it, even to herself, but she would like to be special to some boy. A boy like Bruce.

7

Lisa greeted E.E. enthusiastically on Wednesday morning. "Hi," she said, with a grin that lit up her whole face. "Boy, am I glad to see you."

Elizabeth felt a little awkward after such an exuberant greeting, but Lisa didn't seem to notice. Grabbing E.E.'s hand, she practically dragged her over to the same table where they had sat Monday.

"This is going to be lots of fun. What do we get to talk about today?" Lisa asked. Her brown eyes were fairly dancing with excitement.

"We're not going to talk about anything right now," E.E. said, laying a white sheet of paper on the table. "Miss Kirkpatrick said you're supposed to take this test first. I'll sit here and wait for you while you take it, and if you don't understand something you can ask me about it."

The light in Lisa's eyes seemed to be immediately extinguished. It was as if someone had pulled down a screen in front of her and a different little girl had emerged when the screen was raised. This Lisa appeared sullen and indifferent.

"Take as long as you need," E.E. said, trying to act as if she didn't notice the change, "but try to do your best."

Opening the book in her lap, Elizabeth pretended to read, but all the while she studied Lisa. The little girl picked up her pencil and stared down at the paper. She continued to stare as she turned the pencil over and over, end for end.

Eventually, a dreamy expression came across her face and she gazed out the window. She also found something else to do with the pencil, twisting it around and around in a stray lock of her dark brown hair.

"Don't forget about your test," E.E. reminded her gently.

The dreamy look vanished as Lisa brought the pencil down to her paper and began to write with a stiff and jerky motion. She reminded E.E. of a miniature robot, everything about her seemed so automated and unnatural.

After Lisa had written down a few answers, the whole process started over again, with E.E. having to remind her once more to work on her test instead of staring out the window.

By the time the class period was over, E.E. felt as exhausted as Lisa looked. She took the test paper and promised to see Lisa on Friday.

"Okay," Lisa answered apathetically.

E.E. studied the test thoughtfully as she carried it to Miss Kirkpatrick's office. A few of the simplest problems such as $1 + 1$ and $1 + 2$ were done correctly. But most of the numbers on the page were written backward, and problems such as 5 + 5 were answered "= 01" if they were answered at all.

A sinking feeling seemed to settle in the center of E.E.'s stomach as she entered Miss Kirkpatrick's door. Lisa wasn't dumb, E.E. could tell by looking at the little girl's eyes and listening to her speak. How did you help someone like that?

E.E.'s confidence of Monday night had disappeared, leaving in its place a kind of puzzled helplessness like she'd felt when she first found out about the project.

Everyone else had already assembled in Miss Kirkpatrick's office, and E.E. walked over self-consciously to stand by the other two girls.

"I want each of you to keep the test you administered today," Miss Kirkpatrick said. "I actually had you give them for your benefit rather than the pupil's."

A serious look was on her face as she gazed at each of them in turn. Then she continued, "I know what you've all been thinking since you left Monday and read the paper I gave you: This is so easy it's ridiculous. Why should the school need anyone to help with something like this? It sounds as if they want free babysitters while the regular teachers take a break."

E.E. could feel her face growing hot from embarrassment. She felt as if someone had tape recorded her thoughts the other evening and given the cassette to Miss Kirkpatrick. She couldn't bear to raise her eyes; everyone was probably staring at her red face.

"I can see from the expressions on everyone's faces that I was correct," Miss Kirkpatrick said in a kind voice. "Don't feel badly. That's how everyone is at first. I just wanted you each to realize that this is serious business and not quite so simple as it seems. See you all Friday," she said cheerily.

As they walked out of the grade school, E.E. kept wondering if anyone else felt as exposed as she did, or as helpless, either. Would anything *she* could do really be of that much value?

She kept seeing Lisa with that blank look on her face, but she had such potential, E.E. knew. If only she could find a way to get through to her and make her want to learn.

"You know, we ought to feel privileged." Bruce's voice interrupted her thoughts, and E.E. found herself listening to him with interest. "They've given us a real responsibility. I just hope I'll be able to help Tommy some way."

No one spoke, but most of them nodded their heads in agreement. E.E. didn't think she had ever seen six teenagers so silent and thoughtful before.

Somehow it bothered her that Bruce had been the one to voice his thoughts. The picture she had of him was set as firmly as if it were embedded in concrete, but his actions weren't conforming to that image.

She had dissected and analyzed him, putting him into a category marked "shallow," yet his words just now had revealed a real depth of character.

E.E. was surprised at her reaction to Bruce's words. She was disgruntled and yet in agreement, dismayed yet pleased—she didn't want to admire someone whom she disliked.

But did she really dislike him? She certainly didn't like the way he had tried to treat her. If only . . . oh, well, what was the use of thinking about it? She kicked at a rock in her path on the sidewalk and sent it skittering into the street.

That act broke the spell which held everyone and, with the exception of E.E., they all began to talk again as they returned to the high school.

The difference in Lisa continued to bother Elizabeth for the rest of the day. Lisa had been so alive and animated before the math test. Her sudden blankness had reminded E.E. of empty yards at dusk, when all the children on the block had been called in from play.

She was still thinking about the situation at the dinner table that evening.

"Why so serious, honey?" her father asked, as he settled back with his coffee when the meal was finished.

"I keep thinking about Lisa," E.E. admitted. She propped her chin on her hand and sighed. "I guess I didn't believe any of this was true until today. Then when I saw all those backward numbers, and especially the look on her face . . . I don't know how to explain what I'm trying to say . . ." She gave a helpless shrug before she continued. "I want to do something so badly, but I don't know what."

"I'm glad you feel the way you do," her father said thoughtfully. "You wouldn't be Elizabeth if you didn't."

E.E. knit her brows.

"You're never satisfied to do things halfway," her dad explained. "But I think you're taking this a little too seriously."

Elizabeth opened her mouth to protest, but her father continued, "Just be patient a minute and listen. In the first place, the school evidently has success with its Learning Disability program or they would try something different. Just because you don't understand everything you're doing and why, doesn't mean it won't work."

"I didn't really think of it that way," E.E. conceded. "I guess I was acting as if I were the first person to discover Learning Disabilities. But still, I just feel so inadequate."

"There's nothing wrong with feeling inadequate," her mother said. "In fact, I'd think that would make it more of a challenge."

"You're right," E.E. answered slowly as the wheels in her head began spinning. "Instead of sitting around worrying about the fact that I don't know what I'm doing, I ought to be finding out. I could start by reading all I can about the subject."

"Sounds like a good idea," her father agreed, pushing his chair back from the table.

"There aren't enough teaching aids at the school," E.E. continued in an excited voice. "Maybe I could make some things——" Breaking off in the middle of her sentence, she looked eagerly from her father to her mother. "Could I use the car to go to the shopping center as soon as I get the kitchen cleaned? Will you go with me, Mom?"

"You can use the car," her dad said.

"Why don't you see if Cindy wants to go with you

instead?" her mom asked. "And I'll take care of the kitchen."

E.E. flashed her mother a smile. "Thanks, Mom."

Ten minutes later she and Cindy were driving to Willow Creek Shopping Center.

"What are you going to buy, anyway?" Cindy asked. "You look like a kid with fifty cents to spend in a candy store."

"Actually, I have ten dollars," E.E. said with a grin, "and I'm not sure what I want to get yet. I want to make some kind of learning aid to help Lisa with her math. I thought about using construction paper and poster board, and cutting out some numbers for her to match up, but I need something so they'll stick and still be removable."

"H-m-m," Cindy murmured with a thoughtful expression on her face. "I've got it," she said at last with a smug look.

"So don't just sit there . . . tell me!"

"Use felt instead. Mom does that a lot for her Sunday School class. The felt will stick to itself."

"Sounds perfect," E.E. agreed. "Now if I just have enough money to buy several different colors."

Elizabeth parked in front of a discount store and the two girls walked back to the fabric department. She was disappointed to find only one color of felt, a vivid yellow, but it was the perfect shade for the background, bright enough to be colorful, yet light enough to write numbers on with a marking pen.

"We can look at Ringold's for some other colors," Cindy remarked as they waited for the clerk to cut the fabric.

"If it's more felt you want," the saleslady said,

"you might try the crafts department. Of course, they only have small pieces," she added as she stapled the price to the material.

When they searched through the crafts, E.E. found just what she wanted: a package of felt squares with every color imaginable. Then she got a package of stencils and a magic marker to draw the numbers.

"That looks like it should be everything I need, and it's a good thing. It will probably take every speck of my money."

"Let's get something to drink before we go," Cindy suggested. "I'll buy."

"How can I refuse an offer like that?" E.E. asked as they headed toward the snack area on the opposite side of the store.

"Hey, look," Cindy said when they were almost there. "There's Bruce Johnson with Tammi Smith."

E.E. glanced in the direction her friend had nodded. Sure enough, there was Bruce carrying two cokes as he followed Tammi to an empty booth.

"I'm glad we saw them," E.E. said. "Now maybe you'll quit bugging me about Bruce." Though she spoke quietly, bitterness echoed in her voice and a feeling of despair seemed to climb down into her throat.

8

Elizabeth read thoughtfully over the questions on the physics test that Mr. Creason had just passed out. Every single one was an essay question.

1. What is meant by the tolerance allowed in machine construction?

2. How can a claw hammer exert a pull of half a ton?

3. How would you move a barn with a block and tackle?

4. Which is more important, a large mechanical advantage or a high mechanical efficiency? Explain.

5. When several parallel forces are in equilibrium, (a) how does the sum of the forces acting in one direction compare with the sum of the forces acting in the opposite direction? (b) How does the sum of the moments of the forces tending to produce clockwise rotation about any given point compare with the sum of the moments of the

forces tending to produce counterclockwise rotation about the same point?

There were groans round the room as other kids looked over the test, and E.E. couldn't help feeling a kind of smug satisfaction as she began to write the answers.

They'd gone over everything in class, it was just a matter of studying the material and retaining it. That was exactly what she had done.

Bruce finished right before she did. He carried his test up and laid it on Mr. Creason's desk just as she folded hers lengthwise and wrote her name in the corner.

"I'd like to see you after class today about that project you're working on," Mr. Creason said to Bruce.

"Good," Bruce answered. "I'm excited about it."

After handing in her test, E.E. took out a book to read until class was over, but she couldn't seem to get interested in it.

What kind of project were Mr. Creason and Bruce talking about? She wished there were some way to find out. It was probably something for extra credit. She'd noticed lately how Bruce always had the correct answer if he was called on in class. Maybe he found someone else to help him study, she thought cynically.

E.E. couldn't help smiling when Mr. Creason laid her physics test on the edge of her desk the following Monday. A+—just what she expected, but that didn't make her any less pleased.

Suddenly, a paper fluttered past and landed at her feet. She reached down to pick it up for Mr. Creason, and Bruce Johnson's name caught her eye. Beneath his name was written a large red A+, too.

E.E. felt a strange prickling up and down her spine as she handed the test to the teacher. Bruce Johnson was no dummy! His test proved that. And he couldn't have cheated; it was almost impossible to cheat on essay questions.

She had begun to suspect that he was quite intelligent. She might have realized it sooner, but he kept a low profile and never bragged about his accomplishments like some of the guys did.

She was the dumb one, she realized, as Mr. Creason went to the blackboard and began drawing a diagram to explain balanced couples.

"When two equal parallel forces acting in opposite direction are applied to a body at points some distance apart, they tend to make the body rotate," Mr. Creason was saying. "Such a pair of forces constitutes a couple."

Mr. Creason continued, but E.E. listened as if from a great distance. What constituted a couple in her mind at the moment had nothing to do with physics.

Bruce must actually have asked her to study with him because he liked her, and she had already ruined everything! He didn't even act as if he noticed her any more and she had no one to blame but herself.

That realization continued to plague her through the remainder of the class period.

When the bell rang she followed Bruce and Donna Brown into the hall.

"How did you do on the test?" Bruce asked Donna.

"B—, and I was lucky to get that. How about you?"

"Oh, I did all right," Bruce answered casually. "Maybe we can get together and study for the next test."

"I'd like that," Donna replied, looking up at him with her large violet eyes and fluttering her lashes.

A pang of jealousy stabbed through E.E. at their words, and she slowed her pace. She didn't want Bruce to look around and see her dogging their footsteps and listening to their conversation. Besides that, she didn't want to hear any more.

She had already heard enough to make her miserable. Donna had made a lower grade than Bruce on the test, so he didn't need her help to study for the next one. And he obviously hadn't needed E.E.'s either. It was still hard to believe that he must have really liked her.

She had blown any chance she had with him. Even though she liked him, there was no way she could compete with the girls he was dating now. She wasn't popular and pretty and no way would she go around batting her eyes at a boy regardless of how much she liked him.

Glancing down at her tightly clenched fist, E.E. opened it and stared at the imprint of her nails on the palm of her hand. It was too late to do anything about Bruce and her now. She felt as if her feet were weighted as she walked slowly to meet Cindy at her locker.

Most of the time Cindy rode to and from school with her cheerleading friends, but about once or twice each week she rode the bus with E.E. Since it was so pretty out today, they had already decided to walk home and stop at the drugstore for a coke.

Cindy was already waiting for her. "I thought I might have to send a search party out for you," she said.

"Not this time."

"Hey, why don't we stop at the Snuggle In instead of the drugstore?" Cindy suggested.

E.E. shook her head. "I'd be miserable the whole time. But listen, Cindy, if you wanted to meet someone there or something, I don't mind. I can ride the bus."

"I don't" Cindy said. "We'll go to the drugstore. I just thought maybe it would be good for you to circulate a little more."

"I wish people would let *me* decide what's good for me," E.E. said as she grabbed her armload of books.

"Do you really want to carry all of those across town?" Cindy asked.

"I suppose I don't have to take every single one," E.E. said, putting about half her load back. "Besides, I have plans for tonight. You can't come over for a while, can you?"

"What for?" Cindy asked suspiciously as they started down the hall.

"I never did finish that thing I was making for Lisa. I wanted to get it done so I could take it Wednesday."

"I thought you started working on that as soon as we got back from the store the other day."

"I did, but it took a long time to decide exactly how I wanted to make it, and it's been more work than I expected," E.E. explained. "So, what do you say? Will you help me?"

"Sure," Cindy said. "But you'll have to come to my house. Dad and Mom have to be gone and Dad's expecting an important call that he wants me to take."

As the girls stepped out into the afternoon sunshine, E.E. inhaled deeply.

"It smells like autumn," she said. "Like apples and old leaves."

"You're right," Cindy agreed, wrinkling her nose and sniffing.

They strolled leisurely down the sidewalk, and across the intersection, then several more blocks until they came to the business district of town.

"I'm glad we decided to walk," Cindy said, breaking their compatible silence.

"Me too, although I wouldn't want to walk two miles every day."

Cindy stopped in front of the display window of Jo Carroll's fashions. "Look at that outfit," she said.

"Which one?"

"There," Cindy answered, pointing to a mannequin wearing a light green blouse, kelly green cashmere cardigan, and a plaid wool skirt.

"It looks like it would cost a fortune," E.E. said, "and somehow it doesn't really seem like your type."

"I was thinking about how it would look on you," Cindy said pointedly.

"Too expensive," E.E. mumbled, and started walking again.

"You'd be a knockout in the kelly green with your hazel eyes and brown hair," Cindy said, warming to her subject. "Then you could get your hair cut at Sonia's," she continued, waving her hand in the direction of Sonia's Salon on the opposite side of the street.

"You've got to be kidding," E.E. said, rolling her eyes. "She's the one who styled Miss Oklahoma's hair last year. She'd take one look at me and faint."

"She'd probably consider it one of the greatest challenges of her career," Cindy said with a grin.

"Thanks a lot," E.E. responded, sticking out her tongue.

Both of them were laughing as they entered the drugstore. Most of the booths were empty. They plopped down in the closest one and ordered a Coke.

"Whew," Cindy said, as they sipped their drinks a short while later. "I wouldn't want to walk all that way, if we couldn't stop and cool off."

"Like I said, I wouldn't want to do this every day."

Cindy twirled the ice in the glass with her straw. "Looks like you don't need to worry about Bruce bugging you any more," she said.

E.E. could tell she was choosing her words carefully. "Why's that?" she asked, swallowing hard at the lump in her throat.

"Tammi said he asked her to go to the party after the game this Friday. That makes three dates he's had with her, so it must be serious."

"Maybe to Tammi, but Bruce also asked Donna Brown to study with him sometime."

"How do you know that?" Cindy asked, raising her eyebrows in surprise.

"I heard him after class today."

"Maybe you were right about his trying to get help with his homework. I didn't think so at the time but . . ." she finished her sentence with a shrug.

"I was wrong," E.E. stated bluntly. "He made an A+ on his physics test—all essay questions—and I have a feeling he's super smart."

"Fantastic!" Cindy said, her eyes widening. "Then that means he really did like you, and if he doesn't have a thing for Tammi, maybe it's not too late."

"Guess again," E.E. said mournfully. "You wouldn't believe how rude I was when I said I didn't want to go to the library with him. I even skipped the first meeting of Math Club so I could avoid him. I'm afraid it's a hopeless situation."

9

"Oh, I love it, E.E. Thank you!" Lisa exclaimed. Her brown eyes sparkled as E.E. spread out the felt background and showed her how to match up the different colored felt numbers she and Cindy had cut out.

"You really made it just for me?" Lisa asked again.

E.E. nodded her head for the second time as Lisa impulsively leaned over and kissed her on the cheek.

"What was that for?" E.E. asked in surprise. Her voice felt suddenly sandpapery and she was terribly conscious of her eyes misting over. She'd never been kissed by a child before. In fact, she'd never been kissed by anyone except her parents and her Aunt Jane.

"That's cause you're my best friend," Lisa said emphatically.

"I'm glad," E.E. said, the words catching in her

throat. Embarrassed by her softness, she squared her shoulders and spoke in a firm voice. "We'd better get busy and quit wasting time."

"I'm ready," Lisa said.

E.E. noticed joyfully that for the first time Lisa didn't freeze up when she mentioned getting to work.

"Okay," E.E. said. "I want you to take every number and put it where it belongs. Start with the ones, then go to the twos."

After sorting through the numbers, Lisa picked out a red number one. She studied the large felt background carefully then looked up at Elizabeth.

"There are six ones. How do I know which one to put it on?"

"It doesn't matter. We're going to do them all, anyway."

In a short time Lisa had all the numbers covered with a matching felt number. When she was finished, E.E. had her count how many numbers there were altogether as she took them off. Then they mixed them up and she started all over again.

Lisa worked with determination the whole time they were together. E.E. could hardly believe that she didn't stop to stare out the window or forget what she was doing even once.

"You did great today," she told Lisa when she was ready to leave.

Lisa's answering grin warmed her heart. The rosy glow surrounding E.E. lasted for the rest of the day and into the evening. It was a good feeling to know that she had actually made some progress with Lisa.

That evening after dinner, E.E.'s mother glanced over at her. "I need to run to the store," she said.

"Want me to come with you?" E.E. asked as she speared the last bite of cauliflower on her plate.

"Uh—thanks, honey, but . . . your dad's driving me," her mother said.

"*Daddy's* going with you to a store? How did you manage that?"

"I twisted his arm," Dorothy said, winking at Elizabeth.

"I'm taking her, not going in with her," her father grumbled good-naturedly. "I'll wait in the car."

"Anyway, honey, don't be worried if we're gone for a while."

"Sure, okay," E.E. answered. "I'll take care of this," she said, waving her arm over the table. "Then I have some studying I want to do."

Her parents were ready to leave in a few minutes.

"Have fun on your date," she said as they walked through the kitchen and into the garage a short while later.

I wonder what's with them? E.E. thought as she heard the car start, then back out of the garage and out the drive. It was totally out of character for her father to accompany her mother to town on a weekday, or almost any time as far as that went.

Her mother had acted a little strange when E.E. had volunteered to accompany her. Oh, well, it couldn't be anything important, she decided. At least nothing that she needed to worry about.

Humming to herself, she cleared the table and loaded the dishwasher. She didn't dawdle, but worked with a fervor, anxious to get finished. She wanted to finish her homework as quickly as possible, so she could try to think of something else she could make to help Lisa.

After wiping the table and counters, she dried her hands and headed for her room. She was half finished with her homework which was spread out on her desk. There was still some trig problems to do so she started with them.

Next she took out English Lit. She still had to decide what she was going to write her semester paper on. Mrs. Whitman had asked them to turn in their subjects the next day.

E.E. began drawing doodles on a blank sheet of paper as she considered some different subjects to write about. Then she began to thump her pencil on the desk.

Here she was acting like Lisa. Lisa! That was it, she thought, with satisfaction. Why didn't she think of the idea sooner? She could write her paper about Learning Disabilities. It was something she wanted to know more about, anyway.

By the time E.E. finished her French assignment and her folks still weren't home, she began to wonder about them. It was a good thing her mom had said not to worry or that was exactly what she would be doing.

It was nine o'clock before she heard the gravel crunching as a car drove in. Then the garage door opened and in a short while she could hear her folks coming in the kitchen door.

"Hey," she called, going out to meet them. "What *did* take you so long?"

Her mother came into the living room with a

large box in her hands. "Only this," she said, handing it to Elizabeth.

"Extension I," E.E. said, reading the lettering on the box. "Mom, what have you been buying there? That place is expensive."

"Why don't you open it and see?" her dad asked with a wink.

"Well . . . all right," E.E. answered hesitantly, fumbling with the string as she tried to untie the knot.

"Here," her father said, taking out his pocketknife and cutting it for her.

Somehow, E.E. wanted to see what was in the box and at the same time she didn't. Holding her breath, she pulled off the lid and began folding back the layers of tissue paper. A dress lay buried within its depths.

"For me?" E.E. asked uncertainly.

Her mother nodded. E.E. took the dress out of the box and held it up by the shoulders. It really was lovely.

The fabric was a tiny floral pattern on a background the color of ripe strawberries. A scoop neckline was set off with a lace collar and there was also lace on the flounce at the bottom of the skirt. But the ribbon and lace detailing down the center front to the waist and the sheer long white sleeves seemed to be the things that really made the dress.

"It's beautiful," E.E. said breathlessly. "Thanks, but why . . . ? I mean it's not my birthday or anything."

"You've been working so hard, dear, and you never take the time to go out and buy something for yourself. We just wanted to surprise you," her mother answered. "Now go try it on," she added, with an eager look on her face.

"Okay," E.E. said, trying to feel as excited as her mother seemed to be.

But something wasn't quite right about the whole thing, she decided as she took the dress to her room. For one thing, her mother didn't have the slightest idea what clothes were in now, and yet, she had gone out and purchased a dress that looked like something one of the cheerleaders would wear. Such as Cindy, she thought, pressing her lips firmly together. That was probably who had engineered this whole plan!

After closing the door to her room. E.E. yanked her other clothes off and tossed them on the bed. Everyone kept ganging up on her and she didn't want to be manipulated. They acted as if they had a secret plan called "The Renovation of Elizabeth Ellen Clark."

She couldn't refuse to wear the dress. That would hurt her folks. Besides, she already loved the dress even though she didn't want to. Slipping it over her head, she zipped it up, and turned around to face the mirror. It wasn't exactly a transformation, but it did become her.

So what! She stamped her foot as if that would get rid of some of her frustration. Clothes didn't make a person, and dressing differently wasn't going to change her. Didn't anyone realize that?

Her parents were waiting to see how she looked, she knew. Walking back to the living room, she twirled around once for them, careful not to meet her mother's eyes.

"It's a lovely dress," she said, walking over and giving her mom a squeeze. "I'll wear it to church Sunday."

"I'm glad you like it," her mom said. "You look nice."

Elizabeth felt like a heel as she walked back to her room and changed to her robe. Her mother hadn't even suspected the reason she said she was wearing the dress to church Sunday was because she didn't want to wear it to school.

She had just hung the dress in the closet when there was a knock at her door.

"Come in."

"Hi," Cindy said, walking in the room. "How did your dress fit?"

"I thought you must be involved some way," E.E. said, plopping down in the rocking chair. "It fit perfectly."

"So how do you like it?"

"The dress is fine, it's just the idea that I don't like."

"What idea?" Cindy asked, sitting down on the edge of the bed.

"That everybody's out to change me. I'm tired of it."

"That's not true. They just want to see you develop to your full potential."

"That sounds a little canned," E.E. said, tapping her fingers on the arms of the rocker.

"It is," Cindy agreed with a laugh, "but you know what I mean."

"Not really," E.E. answered with a questioning look on her face.

"I know what you're really like, E., but most of the kids don't. You hide in your drab clothes, and do everything you can to shut people out. You might as well be wearing a sign that says 'Keep Away.'"

"Yes, but the trouble with people," E.E. said slowly, "is that they either swallow you up or reject you if you try to be your own self." She felt as if her ribs were steel bands, squeezing tighter and tighter around her lungs. What she'd said was true, and maybe Cindy would reject her, too, after all these years.

"You're going to be warped for the rest of your life if you don't change your ideas and do something soon," Cindy said, shaking an accusing finger at E.E. "Do you know what people think about you?"

"I'm not sure I want to know."

"They think you're a real snob," Cindy continued, "and *you're* the only one who can change their minds. Nobody else can do it for you."

"So . . . why should I care what they think?" E.E. asked with a shrug.

"See," Cindy said, shaking her finger again. "That's just the kind of attitude I'm talking about. You'd better do something about it while you still can. You were always just shy and withdrawn until last spring. But it's different now, somehow. You're getting cold and hard. Besides that, you do care. I think you care too much!"

After Cindy had gone, E.E. sat in the rocking chair with her face buried in her hands, as silent and motionless as a figurine. Everything Cindy had said was true, she realized.

Tears trickled down between the gaps in her fingers, and she began rocking the chair back and forth with a hypnotic motion.

She did want to change—she really did, but how could she go about taking such a drastic step? It would involve a whole lot more than wearing a new dress to school.

10

"There's someone in my office to see you," Miss Kirkpatrick said to E.E., then she winked at Lisa. "Maybe you'd like to come, too."

"Oh, goody," Lisa said. "Mama said she'd try to come today. She's been wanting to meet you," she told E.E. proudly.

Elizabeth had been wondering what kind of person Mrs. Forrester was, and it looked as if she were going to have a chance to find out. As the three of them walked to the office, E.E. tried to imagine what Lisa's mother would look like.

There was no way she could have dreamed up anyone as beautiful as Mrs. Forrester. Gorgeous was a better description, but it didn't do justice to her looks.

Her golden hair was cut short, emphasizing her high cheekbones and drawing attention to her large brown eyes. She was taller than E.E. and when she came over to take E.E.'s hand, she moved with the liquid grace of a model.

"You must be E.E.," she said, smiling. "I had to meet you since we hear about you constantly."

"Oh, dear," E.E. said. She wagged her finger at Lisa. "What have you been saying about me?"

Lisa grinned, and Mrs. Forrester's tinkling laughter reminded E.E. of a music box. "Don't worry, it's all been good," Mrs. Forrester said. "We were hoping you could join us for dinner Saturday."

"Why, thank you," E.E. said, surprise in her voice. "I really appreciate your asking me." There was some quality this lady possessed which put E.E. completely at ease.

"Wonderful. Why don't you come at six? I'll write down our address for you." Taking out a pad and pen, she bent over Miss Kirkpatrick's desk and wrote down the information, then handed it to Elizabeth.

"That sounds fine," E.E. told her. "I'll see you then."

Mrs. Forrester ruffled Lisa's brown hair and kissed her cheek. "How are you doing, pumpkin? I can't stay long, but Miss Kirkpatrick said I could come see what you're working on."

After Lisa gave her mother a tour of the room where they worked and showed her some of the things they did, their time was up for that day.

It was just as well, E.E. thought. They hadn't made one bit of progress today that she could tell. Lisa was back to staring out the window and playing with her hair. It seemed as if she had taken three steps backward for her one forward last week.

"Your mom is pretty," she told Lisa.

"She's the prettiest Mom in the whole world," Lisa said. "The nicest one, too."

E.E. thought about Lisa's words as she got ready for dinner at the Forrester's Saturday afternoon. It was obvious that Lisa came from a happy family. E.E. had wondered about that. Of course, she hadn't met the rest of them yet.

After showering and shampooing her long hair, she wrapped up in her old robe and blow-dried her hair, admiring the reddish highlights as she ran the brush through it. When it was dry, she pulled it back in the usual way.

After putting on a gray skirt and sweater, she went to study her reflection in the mirror. What was it Cindy had said to her? Something like "You always hide behind your drab clothes." Suddenly it was as though she were looking at another person—a blah one.

"I wouldn't notice me, either," E.E. whispered. She couldn't go to the Forresters' looking like this.

After yanking off the offending clothes, she hung them back in the closet and took out her new dress. In a moment she had slipped it on and was standing before the mirror again.

There was a definite improvement, but it still wasn't enough. Sighing, E.E. lifted her hand and undid the clasp that held her hair. She hated to have her hair down and stringing into her face, but as it fell like a soft shawl around her shoulders, even she had to admit how much better it looked.

Next she took her contacts out of the drawer and removed her glasses. Her fingers felt fumbling and awkward as she inserted her contacts. They were such a nuisance, she never bothered to wear them, but maybe she'd get used to putting them in if she did it more often.

To complete the transformation, E.E. picked up the only lipgloss she owned and applied a light coat. She was amazed at the difference in her appearance. Why, she even felt different, kind of bubbly and excited.

Her father whistled when she walked into the living room, and E.E. could feel her cheeks flushing with pleasure.

"Is this the beautiful young woman who requested a chauffered car this evening?" he asked.

"Oh, Daddy," she said, as her mother entered the room, too.

"Honey, you look wonderful," her mother said.

"Thanks, Mom. Well, I guess we'd better get going," she told her father.

Ten minutes later, he braked the car in front of the long walk that led up to the Forresters' impressive home.

"Thanks, Dad. See you later," she said as she hopped out of the car. Her legs felt as if they had turned to rubber as she followed the walk up to the intricately carved double doors. She hadn't been expecting anything this elaborate, and all the self-confidence she had felt before immediately disappeared. She could almost feel it draining away.

She could see her hand shaking as she reached out to ring the bell. She had no sooner pushed it when the door opened. Lisa was prancing around by a man who had to be her father, they looked so much alike.

"I thought you'd never get here," she said, grabbing Elizabeth's hand. "Daddy, this is E.E."

"Happy to meet you, E.E.," he said, shaking her other hand. He was tall and lean, with dark brown hair the same color as Lisa's.

"I'm glad to meet you, too, Mr. Forrester," E.E. said.

Just then, Mrs. Forrester came in, evidently from the kitchen because she was drying her hands on the apron encircling her slender waist. If it hadn't been for the apron, she would look as if she had just stepped from the pages of a fashion magazine.

"Hi, E.E.," she said. "Come on, everyone. Dinner's ready. And no more of this Mr. and Mrs. Forrester stuff. Just call us Bill and Sonia."

"B-Bill and Sonia?" E.E. said, her voice squeaking.

"Um-hum," she answered with a smile and a nod.

"Oh, no! I mean . . . uh . . . well, I didn't even think about you being *that* Mr. and Mrs. Forrester." E.E. clamped her mouth shut. They were going to think she was ridiculous, babbling on this way, and she didn't want to be rude. She was just so surprised!

"It's all right," Bill said with a grin. "I never bite, and Sonia only does occasionally."

His light-hearted approach eased E.E.'s distress, and she realized that she was smiling back. They were both so friendly and likeable. She would just have to forget that she was eating dinner with an eminent Tulsa surgeon and his wife, the famous hair stylist. It was a good thing she hadn't known what she was getting into ahead of time, or she would never be here.

To her relief, they passed the formal dining room and went out to the kitchen for dinner. Lisa's two brothers were already there, waiting to eat. Bill introduced everyone and the six of them sat down to eat at the large, round table.

"We call this Mexican Dinner," Sonia told Elizabeth. "Let me make your plate for you so you can see how we do it."

She put a scoop of corn chips on E.E.'s plate, followed by a large spoonful of rice. Next came chili, grated cheese, and chopped lettuce and tomatoes. "Now," she said, handing the plate to E.E., "you put on the amount of taco sauce you want, and you're ready to eat."

Soon everyone had their plates full, and was laughing, eating, and talking. It didn't take long before E.E. felt right at home. If anyone had told her a month ago that she would eat dinner with five strangers and enjoy herself, she wouldn't have believed it. Except somehow the Forresters didn't seem like strangers. She even liked the boys, who kept her laughing with tales about their wrestling practice.

When the meal was finished, Bill and the two boys went to the family room to practice some wrestling escapes.

"He was on the wrestling team in college," Sonia explained, "so the boys are always wanting him to help them."

E.E. helped Sonia clear the table, and stack the dishes by the washer.

"Go make sure your room is clean," Sonia told Lisa, "then you can show it to E.E. in a little while."

Lisa rushed out, leaving Sonia and Elizabeth alone

in the kitchen. "Miss Kirkpatrick tells me you're just what Lisa needed. She seems to think you have a special way with her," Sonia said. "Do you think she's doing any better?"

"I don't know," E.E. answered thoughtfully. "Sometimes I think she is, and then other times, like today. . . ." She stopped and shrugged her shoulders. "I just don't know. I've been wishing that I could work with her a couple of evenings a week."

"Oh, E.E., that's wonderful," Sonia said. "Bill and I discussed the same thing, but I didn't want to ask you. I know how busy high school seniors are. We'd pay you for the tutoring, of course."

"No," E.E. said, shaking her head. "I don't want any money."

Sonia looked as if she were about to protest, then changed her mind. "We'll make it up to you some other way, then," she told E.E. at last.

"Please don't," E.E. said. "I want to do it, and I think maybe it's just as good for me."

"What's just as good for you?" Lisa asked, skipping back into the room.

"Lisa!" Sonia admonished. "That's not polite, but since it concerns you, we'll forgive you this time."

"What does?" Lisa asked. Her eyes sparkled with their usual excitement.

"It's a surprise," Sonia said. "I'll let E.E. tell you while you show her your room, then the three of us can talk more about it before she goes home."

"Let's go, then," Lisa said, tugging on E.E.'s arm.

They climbed the broad, curving stairs in the entryway, and Lisa opened the first door on the left side of the hallway.

Everything was pink and ruffles, reminding E.E. of Cindy's room. The bed was made with the spread slightly askew and it was bulging out at the bottom where toys were sticking out in several places. Other than that, things were fairly neat.

"Very pretty," E.E. said.

"There's a lady who comes and cleans the house and cooks during the week," Lisa said, "but Daddy and Mama make us clean our own rooms. They say it's good for us, but I don't think so," Lisa said, wrinkling her nose.

E.E. had to laugh at the expression on her face.

"Now, tell me what the surprise is," Lisa begged. She sat down on the bed and Elizabeth sat beside her.

"I'm going to help you with your math two evenings a week," E.E. said, wondering what Lisa's reaction would be.

"Really?" Lisa asked, her eyes wide.

When E.E. nodded, Lisa threw her arms around her and gave her a big hug. E.E. hugged her back.

"That's super," Lisa said. "I like you. I wish you were my sister. And you know what else?" she hurried on. "I'm gonna do the very best I can for you. I promise I won't look out the windows any more, okay?"

"Good," E.E. answered with a grin. "I think you're going to turn into a butterfly, yet, Lisa."

"What do you mean?" Lisa asked, puckering her brow.

"It's kind of hard to explain, but you know how at first a butterfly is all wrapped up in a cocoon?"

Lisa nodded and E.E. continued. "It doesn't look

like much then, but one day it breaks out and it's beautiful and perfect. You're having a hard time now, but if we keep working, one of these days it's going to all fit together for you and you'll understand numbers and arithmetic. I guess that's not a very good illustration, but do you know what I'm trying to say?"

"I think so," Lisa said solemnly. "Just like you're a butterfly tonight instead of a cocoon like you usually are. You make a pretty butterfly."

"Why, thank you," E.E. said, swallowing hard. She hadn't thought of it in that respect at all, and yet maybe Lisa had understood E.E.'s point better than she did herself.

"E.E.?" Lisa asked, nudging her arm. "Would it be all right if I call you Beth?"

E.E. looked at her curiously. "It's okay if you really want to. But why?"

"I don't like to call you E.E., and besides, Beth sounds more like a butterfly."

11

"I'll be home by noon," E.E. told her mother as she walked out the kitchen door the following Saturday.

Her brown canvas purse was slung over one shoulder, and she carried a notebook in her other arm. Too bad Cindy couldn't go with her, she thought, as she walked to the city bus stop on the corner. Oh, well, she kind of liked being by herself, anyway.

When she arrived at the library, she climbed the stairs and pushed open the glass door. It was almost empty except for the three librarians. That was the main reason she liked to come at this time of day. It was empty like this every Saturday morning, and almost like having your own private library.

E.E. went to the card file first and looked up "Learning Disabilities." She was disappointed to find only four books listed. After writing down the numbers in her notebook, she went over to her favorite place—some desks lining one corner of the farthest wall. It was a nice, secluded spot to study.

After placing her notebook on one of the desks, she tore out the page she had written on and went to look for the books she had jotted down. One of them was checked out and the three that were left didn't look too promising, she thought, as she carried them back to her seat.

She sat down, wishing she had fastened her hair back this morning. She had left it down a couple of times since Lisa's remark last Saturday, but she didn't know why she'd done so today. She looked through her purse, but there was nothing in it she could use for a tie. If she got desperate enough, she could always ask the librarian for a rubber band.

The books she had looked like some of the oldest ones in the library. After checking the copyright in each one, she decided maybe they were. Two of them were dated 1954 and the other 1942. She doubted if she would glean any useful information from anything so old, but since she had all morning, she might as well glance through them.

She had been reading only a short while when she was conscious of a familiar voice.

"Not one of those books is here."

It was Bruce Johnson! What was *he* doing here? A funny hot and cold feeling tingled up and down E.E.'s spine.

"They may have been put in the wrong place. Why don't you look over the shelves in this area?" the librarian said, "and I'll go see if the books have been checked out."

For the first time that she could remember, E.E. was thankful her hair was down. Bending her head even lower over the book she was reading, she shook it slightly, making her hair fall like a curtain around the sides of her face. Now maybe Bruce wouldn't recognize her if he walked around the bookshelf.

It wasn't that she didn't want to see him. It would be a different matter if she could expect him to say something like, "Why Elizabeth, imagine meeting you here. Why don't you come sit at a table with me and we'll study together?"

That wasn't what would happen, though. Bruce would merely look through her, or at best nod in her direction, and she couldn't stand that. No, it would be better if he didn't recognize her at all.

The librarian returned and E.E. heard her talking to Bruce once more.

"Only one of the books is checked out," she said. "Either someone in the library is reading the others right now, or they've been carried off."

"Thanks for checking," Bruce said. "I can't imagine anyone carrying off three books about Learning Disabilities. I'll look around and see if I can find out who is reading them and ask to use them next."

"If I can help you with anything else, let me know."

E.E. felt rooted to the chair, as if she were part of the same piece of wood it had been made from. Bruce was looking for the books that were laying on the desk in front of her! What was she going to do?

She didn't want to rush over and take him the books. Then he would know that she had been listening to him. Neither did she want to sit there until he came searching for the books and found them with her.

Quickly, she stacked them on the seat between her

and the wall. A moment later, she could hear Bruce's footsteps as he rounded that aisle of books. Then he was standing by her side.

"Excuse me," he said in a polite voice.

Taking a deep breath, E.E. glanced up at him. Her heart was fluttering like a bird with a broken wing.

"Oh, Elizabeth. Sorry, I didn't know it was you."

He didn't say anything else before he walked on, and E.E. felt strangely relieved and let down at the same time. It was what she had expected. As soon as Bruce disappeared around another row of books, E.E. hopped up. She took the books she had been looking at and replaced them on the shelf. He'd find them if he looked again.

She had to get out of here, she decided. She certainly didn't want to keep bumping into Bruce all morning. She could come back some other time to see if there were any information on microfilm.

The wind had switched to the north while she was in the library, and E.E. shivered against its briskness as she stepped outside.

As usual, she had acted like an idiot. She felt like kicking herself all the way to the bus stop instead of walking. She could have told Bruce that she couldn't help hearing him. Then she could have smiled and handed him the books. But, no, she had overreacted and ran out of the library!

What was wrong with her, anyway? It wasn't just the wind chilling her to the bones, she decided as she stepped into the cavelike protection between the two display windows of City Drug to wait for the bus.

Idly, she let her eyes wander over the articles in the window. One item caught her attention. "Quizmo," the box read, "The Bingo Game you play with numbers."

Entering the warm store, she asked the sales clerk to let her see the game. The instructions were almost identical to Bingo, but instead of calling out letters, a person would call out problems such as two plus two. If a player had a four on their card, they could place a chip on the answer.

The price, which had been $7.95, was reduced to $2.95. E.E. felt like someone who had discovered a nugget when they weren't even panning for gold. She paid the clerk and walked out the door with her treasure just as the bus pulled to a stop at the curb.

Thinking about Lisa helped to take her mind off Bruce. She would mentally go through what she hoped to accomplish with Lisa this coming Tuesday and Thursday evenings, as she rode home. That way she wouldn't have an opportunity to think about what had happened at the library.

Better yet, she would write a lesson plan down in her notebook. She surely couldn't think about anything else if she were doing that! Taking out a pencil, she began to jot: Tuesday evening—teach Lisa to play Quizmo. Also work with——

The bus pulled away from the corner and E.E. had to stop writing. She certainly hadn't found out anything about Learning Disabilities this morning. Those books were practically relics. Was Bruce as disappointed as she when he discovered them?

Berating herself for her wandering thoughts, she started to write again, finishing the sentence she had started, ". . . tracing and copying two-digit numbers."

This time the bus lurched to a stop, forcing her to quit writing once more.

Why was Bruce wanting to read those books, too? Maybe he was hoping to find more ways to help Tommy. Probably so, knowing Bruce.

E.E. snapped her notebook shut and put her pencil away. This wasn't keeping her mind off Bruce at all. It seemed to be making matters worse.

Finally she took Quizmo out of the white "City Drug" sack, and looked it over carefully. Lisa would enjoy this, she knew.

Lisa was every bit as excited with the game Tuesday evening as Elizabeth hoped she would be. Maybe that was one reason she enjoyed Lisa so much. Even though she had almost anything a child could want, she still had an unspoiled quality about her. She had a sense of wonder and pleasure about everything, and could get as excited about a simple game as if it were the first and only toy she had ever received.

E.E. was working with Lisa in the kitchen that evening when Sonia walked in.

"Sorry to interrupt you two," she said. "Bill's been called out on an emergency operation. He was supposed to take the boys to wrestling, but I'll have to. I'll be right back."

"If you want to stay and watch them, Lisa and I will be fine. I don't mind staying a little longer," E.E. said.

"Well . . . ," Sonia said. "They have been wanting me to watch them sometime, but. . . ."

"But what?" Lisa questioned.

"I don't want you to have to babysit besides tutor," Sonia said, looking at E.E.

"I'm not a baby," Lisa said in her most grown-up-sounding voice.

"I don't mind," E.E. said with a smile. "I wouldn't have suggested it if I did."

"In that case, I think I will. The boys will be thrilled. Help yourself to anything in the refrigerator while I'm gone."

Ten minutes later, E.E. and Lisa were alone in the large house.

"This is really like being sisters," Lisa said with a big grin, the moment her mother left.

"Yes, I guess so," E.E. agreed. "And of course you know that little sisters always mind their big sisters." It might be a good idea to inject that bit of information.

After they played two more games of Quizmo, Lisa traced numbers, then copied them for twenty minutes.

"That's really good," E.E. said when she finished. "You only made four numbers backward."

"Then can I stay up and wait for Mama and the boys with you?"

"What time do you usually go to bed?" E.E. asked.

"Well . . . uh . . . whenever I want to," Lisa answered in a bright voice.

"Lisa! I don't believe that. Tell me the truth," E.E. said firmly.

"Nine o'clock," Lisa said, wrinkling her nose, "but I'm sure Mama won't care if I stay up one time."

"It's a school night," E.E. reminded her, looking at

her watch. "And you've got just enough time to take your bath."

"Do I hafta?" she whined.

E.E. nodded her head. "Remember, little sisters always mind their big sisters."

"I forgot," Lisa answered in a happier tone. "If I hurry, will you read me a story?"

"It's a deal," E.E. said.

When Sonia, Jeff, and Brett arrived home at 9:15, Lisa was already asleep.

"I can't believe it," Sonia said when E.E. told her. "She usually gives her babysitters a hard time. That's why I didn't even suggest that you try to get her to bed. You must have had a lot of experience."

"I've never babysat before in my life," E.E. admitted.

"Well, I think I'll hire you from now on. Let's see," Sonia said. "I usually pay my sitters a dollar fifty an hour. You were here——"

"No," E.E. interrupted. "I was helping Lisa study and I already said I wouldn't take any money for that."

"All right for this time," Sonia said, "but I won't have you stay again unless I can pay you. Besides," she added with a twinkle in her eyes, "I know just what I can do to show our appreciation for everything you've done for Lisa."

12

"Telephone, Elizabeth," her mother called from the hall on Thursday.

E.E. raised her eyebrows in surprise. The only person who ever called her was Cindy, and she wasn't home this afternoon. E.E. was home herself because of a teacher's meeting Thursday and Friday.

Hopping up from the sofa, E.E. went to the phone, still wondering who could be calling her.

"Beth, this is Sonia. Could you come down to the salon for a while and entertain Lisa until I close?"

"Sure," E.E. said. Sonia had followed her daughter's example in calling E.E. "Beth," and she found she liked it. "I'll have to catch a bus, but it shouldn't take me too long."

"Great. You're a lifesaver!"

E.E. hung up the phone, glad that she had something different to do. Evidently Sonia couldn't find anyone to watch Lisa during the teacher's meeting. She should have known she could have asked E.E.

Or maybe she had just decided to take Lisa along to the salon as a treat and she had gotten bored.

Whatever, she didn't have any other plans, so she didn't mind helping out. It would be kind of interesting to see the inside of the famous Sonia's Salon anyway.

E.E.'s cheeks were pink from the cold by the time she arrived at the salon about thirty minutes later. She opened the door and a glass wind chime tinkled softly.

The salon was fashionable, with two mirrored walls and the other painted a pale mauve. She felt as if she were sinking into the thick, cream-colored carpet as she stepped in the door. To her surprise, no one was there except Sonia and Lisa.

"Surprise!" Lisa yelled. She was bubbling over with excitement and kept hopping from one foot to the other.

"What's all this about?" E.E. asked, lifting curious eyes to Sonia's.

"I promised Lisa she could tell you," Sonia said with a conspiratorial wink.

"Mama's gonna give you your own special hairstyle just like she did for Miss Oklahoma. Isn't that super?"

E.E. didn't know what to say. She felt as if she had been struck dumb. "B-but. . . ." she finally managed.

"No buts about it," Sonia said. "You do all you can to help Lisa, and won't accept one penny for it. It's time you let us do something for you."

E.E. started to say that really wasn't what was bothering her. Then she looked at Lisa, still hopping around with anticipation. Even Sonia's eyes were sparkling with pleasure.

Suddenly E.E. understood that they wanted to do something for her because she was their friend, not because they wanted to change her. It would be thoughtless to spoil their happiness. Regardless of how she felt about having her hair styled, she had to accept or hurt two people she really cared about.

"Aren't you happy?" Lisa asked.

Sonia was beginning to look concerned, as if perhaps she had done the wrong thing.

"I'm very happy," E.E. said, meaning every word. "I'm just not used to surprises."

"Good because we've got——"

"Lisa," Sonia said, interrupting her daughter. "Why don't you get out the shampoo and cream rinse for me?"

"Is there any particular style you have in mind?" Sonia asked as she shampooed E.E.'s hair.

"I can't stand my hair in my eyes," E.E. said "Other than that, I don't really care."

"Good, that's what I was hoping," Sonia said. "I have something perfect in mind. It will be easy for you to learn to take care of, too."

After Sonia washed E.E.'s hair, she transferred her to another chair and brushed her hair, then clipped it up by sections and started cutting.

She worked quickly, but meticulously. E.E. was relieved that she cut it shoulder length. Then she cut some long bangs, explaining that she was feathering them and that they would be curled back out of her face.

When she was finished, she towel-dried E.E.'s hair

some more and blow-dried it. After that, she used a curling iron.

Elizabeth stared at her reflection in wonder when Sonia was finished. Her hair wasn't that different, and yet it was. Somehow the fuller style and fluffiness of the bangs, which were brushed back from her forehead, completely transformed her thin, serious face.

Why, I could actually be pretty, she thought in amazement. "I love it, Sonia," she exclaimed.

Lisa had sat still the whole time, but now she started wiggling in her seat. "Can I get it now, Mama?" she asked at last.

Sonia nodded, and Lisa rushed into a back room and returned immediately, carrying a large gift wrapped in gold foil paper and tied with a white velvet ribbon. She came over and dropped it ceremoniously in E.E.'s lap.

"For me?" E.E. asked.

"Uh-huh," Lisa said. "Mama let me help her pick it out."

"But you shouldn't get me anything," E.E. protested. "You've already given me this fantastic hairstyle, and——"

"Open it," Sonia said sternly. "I wanted to pay you for tutoring and babysitting, but no . . . you wouldn't hear of it, so I don't want to hear another objection."

"All right," E.E. answered meekly, but she almost protested again when she opened the gift. It was the same green outfit Cindy had stopped to admire the day they walked home from school, and E.E. knew it had to have cost a fortune.

Still, it *was* beautiful. "How can I thank you?" she asked, rubbing the softness of the cashmere against her cheek. Her words caught in her throat, not because of the gift, but because of the love behind it.

"It's perfect for your coloring," Sonia said with a pleased smile. "I knew when I saw it in the shop window, it was made just for you."

"Are you going to wear it to school Monday?" Lisa asked, bringing E.E. back to earth.

E.E. hesitated for only a moment. "Of course I am, as long as it isn't hot outside."

"Then I'll pray for it to be cold," Lisa said seriously.

Elizabeth had just put on her new outfit that evening and showed her parents when she saw Marsha Thompson drop Cindy off at her home.

Mrs. Morris answered the door when E.E. knocked a few moments later.

"Why, Elizabeth," she said with a surprised look on her face. "What have you done to yourself? I hardly recognized you, you look so stunning."

"Thanks, Mrs. Morris."

"Cindy's in her room. Go on back."

Cindy was sitting at her dressing table and didn't notice E.E. until she spoke. When she glanced up and saw her in the mirror, she twirled around on her seat and stared at her in obvious amazement.

"I can't believe it! You look fantastic . . . really fantastic."

"What do you mean you can't believe it?" E.E. asked with a laugh. "You're the one who was always trying to convince me I had possibilities. *Remember?*"

"Sure, but I'd about given up hope. I didn't think you would ever do anything." Cindy stood up and walked slowly around E.E., examining her from every angle. "Your hair is marvelous and I told you that outfit was made for you. I'm glad you finally took my advice about something."

E.E. laughed again. Why tell her that wasn't exactly what had happened? "As a matter of fact," E.E. said, sitting down on the bed, "I came over for some more of your good advice."

"Cindy's Suggestions at your service," Cindy quipped, sitting down cross legged on the floor.

"I want to buy a few things. I thought maybe you'd go along and help me pick them out."

Cindy nodded. "You know I will. What do you have in mind?"

"I have to get a curling iron, the kind with bristles on it like a brush, and I thought I'd buy some makeup." E.E. knew she was blushing, but she couldn't help it. She was grateful that Cindy didn't tease her about it.

"You don't need much," Cindy said. "You have a perfect complexion. With a little blush and some lip gloss, you'll be in great shape. And, of course, some mascara for special occasions."

"I wish," E.E. whispered to herself.

"Wish what?" Cindy asked.

"That I'd have some special occasions."

"Don't worry. You will," Cindy said confidently. "Hey, Mom was going to run into the mall this evening. Why don't we go with her and get your stuff?"

"Okay," E.E. agreed. "Lisa's going somewhere with her family tonight and I won't be working with her."

"I'll go tell Mom we're going along while you run over and get your purse."

It didn't take long for the two of them to spend E.E.'s money once they got to the mall.

"If that curling iron hadn't been on sale, I wouldn't have had enough money," E.E. said after they paid for her purchases. "If I keep spending money the way I have been, I'm going to have to start babysitting or something."

"That *would* be the day," Cindy said.

"I'm serious," E.E. said. "I'm already going to stay with Lisa and her brothers tomorrow because of the teachers' meeting."

E.E. enjoyed watching the look of surprise that stole over Cindy's features. "When you decide to change, you certainly aren't half-hearted, are you?" Cindy said.

When they arrived back at Cindy's house, E.E. put on some of the makeup she had bought.

"Sensational," Cindy said. "I want you to look just like this when you go to school Monday."

E.E. shook her head slowly.

"What do you mean, no?" Cindy practically shouted.

"I'm going to wear my contacts Monday instead of my glasses," E.E. answered casually.

"In that case, all right," Cindy said with a grin.

That evening before she got ready for bed, E.E. stood for a long time in front of her mirror. It was hard to believe that she was really the girl in the mirror. She looked attractive and she already enjoyed looking that way.

Maybe she would really turn into the kind of butterfly she and Lisa had been talking about. If only she didn't have to wait for the following Monday to let everyone see the new E.E.

That thought immediately deflated E.E. and she backed up and sat down on the edge of her bed. Leaning her elbows on her knees, she propped her chin in her hands.

Looking like a butterfly and acting like one were two different things. A person could change their looks completely in almost no time at all, but it wasn't so easy to change a whole personality.

She realized that she had changed considerably since the beginning of school. Lisa had seen to that in her own uninhibited way. E.E. had been too self-contained and indifferent to others. Now she was finally beginning to see that other people really needed her.

It was amazing what a simple equation she had discovered: When you start being concerned about other people, you don't have time to worry so much about yourself.

She needed people, too. She could finally admit that. But how could she go about showing people that she wanted to be different than she had been for so long?

13

The jangling alarm woke E.E. an hour earlier than usual on Monday morning. She wanted to have plenty of time to get ready for school. Reaching over, she pushed in the button on the clock, then hopped out of bed. She already felt wide awake, like a child on Christmas morning.

After washing her hair, E.E. began to work with it, doing exactly as Sonia had taught her. She felt awkward as she blow-dried and brushed it at the same time, and even more clumsy as she fumbled around with the curling iron, but every hair fell perfectly into place.

If anyone had told her a few months ago that she would be doing this, she would have thought they were crazy. Now here she was, and she was even enjoying fussing with her appearance!

Next, she put in her contacts. She still liked her glasses. They would be good for a more serious look, but that wasn't what she wanted to achieve today.

She applied a touch of blush to her cheeks and some lip gloss, and she was all set.

When she was finished dressing, Elizabeth thoughtfully studied her image in the mirror. It was impossible, but she looked even better than she had Thursday evening.

She had pizzazz this morning, a kind of sparkle that originated somewhere deep inside and spread outward to her pink cheeks and hazel eyes, even, it seemed, to the shine of her fashionable hair.

After she had picked at her breakfast, she stopped at Cindy's and they walked to the bus together.

"I'm glad you were willing to ride the bus," she told Cindy as they waited at the corner. "I needed someone to bolster my self-confidence."

"The way you look today, it will be all the other girls who will need confidence."

"I appreciate that, but I'm still the same old E.E. Looks don't have much to do with it."

"Oh, I don't know," Cindy said. "It's a good start."

When the bus stopped for them and they climbed aboard, Elizabeth could feel everyone staring at her. She tried to keep a smile on her face, but it felt tight and as unnatural as if her face were encased in plaster.

There was a whistle from the back of the bus, and somehow she knew it was meant for her. She could feel her face growing hot and knew it must be as red as the leaves on the nearby maple tree.

They took a seat, and Ralph Patterson, who was sitting across the aisle, turned his head and nodded at them. "Hi, Cindy," he said. "Hi, E.E. You look great this morning."

"Th-thanks," she stammered.

"Keep smiling," Cindy whispered, nudging her. "After a few days, everyone will be used to the new you and you won't feel so conspicuous."

E.E. hoped Cindy knew what she was talking about, but as the day wore on, she couldn't help doubting that people would ever get used to her.

Everyone kept complimenting her, even kids she barely knew. She felt so bungling and awkward when she tried to reply pleasantly. Maybe it would be better to look like she had before, but she knew she didn't mean it. She enjoyed looking her best.

What would Bruce think when he saw her? she wondered as activity period approached. How nice it would be if they crashed into each other today, but things like that happened only when you didn't want them to.

When the time came to go over to the grade school, Elizabeth walked with the other two girls. She was surprised at how disappointed she felt when she noticed that the boys were already far ahead of them. When she wanted to keep out of Bruce's way, she ran into him all the time.

"Boy, you really look super today," Rita said, interrupting E.E.'s thoughts. "I love your haircut."

"Thanks," E.E. murmured for what felt like the hundredth time that day. If she could just think of something else to say to everyone so they would know she wanted to be friendly.

Well, why not try? She could start by being honest with her feelings. "It's kind of new for me," she said slowly. "You girls look great all the time. Maybe you could give me a few ideas."

Both of the girls smiled and E.E. could tell she had said the right thing.

"Of course we will," Rita said. "Won't we, Sheryl?"

The petite redhead nodded her agreement. "Sure, but you'll have to give us a for instance."

E.E. swallowed in surprise. She hadn't expected this much enthusiasm, and she wasn't prepared with an answer. "Um . . . well . . . like my clothes," she said, hesitating. "I can't afford to just go out and buy all new things, and the ones I have are pretty blah."

"That's no problem," Rita said. "Your clothes are basically fine, if you just dress them up with a few bright colors."

"Why don't we come over one evening?" Sheryl suggested. "We'll go through your wardrobe and the three of us can decide exactly what you need."

"That sounds great," E.E. said. Her face felt as if the plaster had been chipped away as she smiled happily.

"You'll probably be surprised at how little you really need to buy," Sheryl continued enthusiastically. "A new belt or scarf can work wonders."

"Why don't we come over this evening?" Rita said. "That way we won't waste any time."

"I'll ask Cindy to come over, too," E.E. said.

"I'd like to come," Sheryl said, looking at both of them and frowning, "but I've got this algebra assignment that my brother will have to help me with."

"Bring it along," E.E. said. "I'll help you if you want me to."

"Okay. Thanks a lot."

A warm sense of satisfaction enveloped E.E. as she walked along with her two new friends. It was a kind of cozy, contented feeling, like walking into the kitchen when her mother was baking.

The remainder of the school day seemed to alternate between speeding and crawling by. Everyone was so friendly about commenting on her appearance, E.E. felt almost as if she were a new girl at school. In a way, maybe that's what she was. No one seemed to mind that she didn't always know what to say and sometimes all she did was smile.

Would everything really be back to normal in a few days like Cindy had said? And what about Bruce? she kept thinking. Would he notice a difference?

He was already sitting in his seat when E.E. walked into physics. He looked up from his desk as she passed, and E.E. did her best to give him a friendly smile.

"Hi," he said, and nodded.

Oh, well, E.E. thought with the barest whisper of a sigh as she scooted into her seat. What did she expect? Bruce wasn't going to start automatically acting friendly just because other people did. He would have to realize that she was genuinely trying to change, and even then it might not do any good. There wasn't any reason why he should start liking her again.

Bruce tapped her on the shoulder, and E.E. could feel her pulse racing as an odd zingy feeling inched up her spine. Drawing a long, pulsating breath, she made herself count to three before she turned around. He probably only wanted to borrow some paper or something, and she didn't want him to know how much his touch had affected her.

"You look nice today," he whispered.

A deep sense of pleasure filled E.E.'s heart and lifted it up until she felt as if she were floating. Her "Thanks" got caught in her throat and all she could do was smile again.

Maybe, just maybe, things weren't so hopeless after all. That possibility made the plans to work on her wardrobe this evening even more exciting.

Cindy came early that night, and exactly at seven-thirty the other two girls arrived.

"Your exterior decorators have arrived," Rita said when E.E. opened the door.

"You may feel as if you've taken on an impossible job," E.E. said with a laugh.

"I doubt it," Sheryl said.

"Challenging maybe, but not impossible," Rita teased.

After E.E. introduced the girls to her parents, the three of them went back to her room. Cindy was already digging clothes out of the closet and laying them on the bed.

"Good grief," E.E. said, staring at the pile of clothes. "I didn't know you were going to take this quite so seriously."

"Of course we are," Cindy said. "The three of us have already discussed this project. We want to do the best job possible."

"That's right," Sheryl agreed. "Now first of all I need a paper and pencil to write everything down."

"Here you are," Rita said, pulling a sheet of paper

out of her notebook and handing it to Sheryl along
with a pencil.

"This is everything," Cindy said, staggering
beneath another load of clothes. She dumped them
on the bed and stood back with her hands on her
hips to survey her masterpiece.

E.E. sat down in the rocking chair and stared at
the mess. "I really didn't want to clean out my closet
tonight," she moaned. "I mean . . . couldn't we
just have scooted my things back and forth on the
rod to check them over?"

"Too late now," Rita observed.

"All four of us couldn't fit into your closet. It will
be quicker this way," Cindy said. "Don't worry, I'll
help you put everything back."

Sheryl sat down at E.E.'s desk and spread out the
piece of paper with a flourish. "Okay," she said with
her pencil poised. "I'm ready." She looked as serious
as a court stenographer, and the other three girls
laughed.

"Why don't you make one list of outfits and another of accessories needed for each one," Cindy
suggested.

"Sounds like a good idea," Sheryl said, writing
down the headings at the top of the page.

"Actually, you're in pretty good shape," Rita observed, starting to lay all the skirts in one pile.
"Earth tones are the "in" thing this year, and you've
got lots of those."

Forty-five minutes later, the clothes were in neat
stacks, and Sheryl had a long list of items such as:
gold mesh belt, brown leather belt, bolo tie, black

grosgrain ribbon, candy-apple-red scarf, and peacock-blue scarf.

Then Rita and Cindy volunteered to put the clothes away while E.E. helped Rita with her algebra assignment.

Just as everyone finished, there was a light tap on the door. "Anyone hungry?" E.E.'s mother asked. "You girls have been in there over an hour. There are snickerdoodles and hot chocolate in the kitchen when you're ready."

"M-m-m," Sheryl said. "We picked the right place to come to. What are we waiting for?"

"Wait," Rita said. "We forgot one thing. What about the Harvest Ball?"

"What about it?" Cindy and Sheryl asked in unison.

"Do you have anything you can wear to it?" Rita asked, turning to E.E.

"Well . . . no," E.E. mumbled, "but I won't be going anyway. In the first place, no one would ask me, and in the second place, I don't even know how to dance if they did."

"That's a defeatist attitude," Rita said. "We can teach you how to dance."

"That's right," Sheryl said, "and surely there's someone you wouldn't mind going with."

"There is someone," Cindy told them. "He's a super neat guy, too. I wouldn't mind going with him myself."

"Wow! He must be something," Rita said.

"He is," E.E. admitted, "but he would never invite me to the Harvest Ball."

14

"You're a lifesaver, Beth," Sonia said when she opened the door for Elizabeth Tuesday evening. "Just don't forget, it's a paid job when you babysit, too."

"Okay," E.E. agreed.

"Hi, Beth," Lisa said, running out to the entry-way. "O-o-oh," she said, pouching out her bottom lip. "How come you wore your glasses? You look prettier without them."

"Lisa!" Sonia reprimanded.

"It's all right," E.E. said. "I wore these so I would look strict, young lady," she said, shaking her finger at Lisa. "Then I thought you might get down to business and quit goofing around."

"You still look like a butterfly. Doesn't she, Mama?"

When Sonia cocked her head slightly and studied her for a moment, E.E. could feel her cheeks growing pink.

"You're right. She does," Sonia said with a smile. "I'll be back by nine-thirty," she told E.E.

As soon as Sonia left, E.E. and Lisa went into the family room to study.

"Do you have a boyfriend?" Lisa asked as E.E. opened the Quizmo box.

"You shouldn't be so nosy," E.E. said. "I came here so we could study, not so you could ask me a bunch of questions."

"I'm sorry. I just wanted to know 'cause I like you," Lisa said in a plaintive voice. Her big brown eyes looked sad and E.E. could feel her resistance melting.

"Forget it," E.E. said, ruffling Lisa's short hair. "Now let's get busy."

"Okay," Lisa answered meekly.

"Ten plus two."

"Twelve," Lisa said, covering the number on her Quizmo card with a round wooden disk.

"Eight plus three."

"Eleven."

"Four plus five."

"Nine."

"Great," E.E. said.

She gave Lisa all the problems in the game. Lisa quizmoed several times and didn't miss one.

"We might as well go on to something else," E.E. told her. "You did that perfectly. I'll draw some numbers for you to copy. After that, I'll write some problems and you can write the answers."

Taking a sheet of second grade lined paper, E.E. printed all the numbers from one through twenty, and handed the paper to Lisa.

Lisa studied the page for a short while, then with out hesitating, carefully copied each number in another line.

"There," she said, giving the page back to Eliza beth.

"Good," E.E. said, after glancing over it. "Now we'll see how you do on something harder."

This time she wrote down addition problems which required two-digit answers. That kind of problem usually caused Lisa to daydream.

To E.E.'s amazement, that didn't happen this eve ning. Lisa began to work slowly, but steadily. Since she didn't play with her pencil or stop to look around the room, she finished the problems in record time.

"Lisa, that's wonderful," E.E. said after she checked the answers. She felt as proud as if she were Anne Sullivan teaching Helen Keller. "You didn't make one mistake," she said, giving Lisa a hug.

"I knew I wouldn't," Lisa stated proudly.

"But why?" E.E. questioned. "What's different now than it used to be?" Somehow she felt that if Lisa could answer her question, maybe E.E. would discover something which would help other children with the same problem.

Lisa shrugged. "I don't know. I was scared before."

"You're not any more?" E.E. asked.

"Sometimes I am and sometimes I'm not," Lisa ex plained, "but I wanted to do it right tonight and I forgot to be scared."

"Why did you want to do it right tonight?"

" 'Cause one time you said that whenever I did all

the problems right, we could do whatever I wanted to for the rest of the evening."

Searching her memory, E.E. recalled the moment that Lisa was talking about. "That's right, I did. So what do you want to do, play a game? Read a book? You name it."

"I just want to talk," Lisa said. "Every time I try to talk, you say we have to get busy."

"Fine," E.E. said, settling back comfortably into the corner of the sofa. "What do you want to talk about?"

"I want to know if you have a boyfriend," Lisa said with a mischievous gleam in her eyes.

Even though she felt like shaking Lisa, she couldn't help laughing. "You're sneaky, do you know that? And, no, I don't have a boyfriend. Now are you satisfied?"

"That's too bad. But don't worry, I bet you'll get one since you're so pretty."

"Who says I'm worried?" E.E. asked with a smile.

"Aren't there any nice boys in your school?"

"Of course there are, silly."

"Are any of them in your classes?"

"Yes," E.E. said. "There's one really nice boy who sits behind me in physics class."

"What's his name?" Lisa asked with sparkling eyes.

"Just never mind," E.E. said, pretending to frown fiercely. "I'm not going to tell you another thing."

"Why not?" Lisa asked, pouting. "I thought we were friends."

"Oh, for goodness sake," E.E. said in exasperation. "His name is Bruce. Now, what game do you want to play?" she added quickly before Lisa had a chance to ask any more questions.

"Uno," Lisa answered promptly.

Later that evening, after E.E. had put Lisa to bed, she reviewed their conversation. Funny kid, she thought, smiling to herself. Lisa really was almost like having a kid sister—pesky, but sweet.

Still, E.E. could have kicked herself for telling Lisa anything about Bruce. Not that it would matter, but Lisa would probably bug her about Bruce from now on.

She took out her trig and started working on it. She only had three problems to do, and just as she finished, Sonia arrived home with the boys.

"Baths and bed right now," Sonia told them the moment they were in the house. "It's later than usual and I don't want you two falling asleep in school tomorrow."

Neither Jeff nor Brett protested as they headed for the stairs.

"Why don't you have a cup of spice tea with me before you go home?" Sonia asked E.E.

"I'd like that," E.E. answered, following Sonia out to the kitchen.

"Lisa did all her work perfectly this evening," E.E. told Sonia as she prepared their tea. "She's gradually improving, but this is the best she's done."

"I give her tutor a lot of credit," Sonia said with a smile. "You've been wonderful for her."

"Miss Kirkpatrick said motivation can make a big difference. I'm not any expert, but I think that applied in Lisa's case. I don't know that I had that much to do with it, but she's been wonderful for me," E.E. said.

Sonia carried the two steaming cups over to the table and sat down across from E.E. "I've noticed quite a change in you since the first evening you had dinner with us, but I don't understand what Lisa had to do with it."

"She has this sense of wonder that makes me notice things, too. Only she's had such a block when it comes to math, it's almost as if she were a different little girl."

"What you've said is true," Sonia agreed, "but I still don't see how that helped you."

"I guess it was just that when I finally started worrying about helping someone else, I didn't have so much time to worry about myself."

"When Lisa mentioned you looked like a butterfly this evening, she didn't realize there was a lot more than appearance involved. You've really blossomed in the last few weeks." Suddenly Sonia laughed. "You would have choked Lisa if you could have heard her before you came."

"She wasn't happening to wonder if I have a boyfriend, was she?"

"Oh," Sonia said. "So she did pester you about it, after I warned her not to."

"It's all right, I already choked her," E.E. said with a laugh. "Really, when I told her I don't have a boyfriend, there wasn't too much more she could ask."

"I didn't have a boyfriend when I was your age, either," Sonia said. "Everyone else did, but I was so shy I couldn't even say my name if a boy asked me."

"You, shy?" E.E. asked in surprise.

"Hard to believe, isn't it?"

When E.E. nodded, Sonia went on to explain. "Finally, toward the end of my senior year, I decided I had as much going for me as anyone else. I just had to act like it. The amazing thing was, it worked. The boy I'd secretly had a crush on all year even asked me to the prom."

"It doesn't seem as if you could have ever been shy," E.E. said.

"It's similar to what you were talking about concerning Lisa. I was like you. When I finally showed some interest in other people, I forgot to worry about myself, too. Now I try to decide how I can put someone else at ease instead of the other way around."

"I wonder if that would work for me," E.E. said, turning the cup of tea slowly in her hands, as the warmth spread through her fingers.

"But it's already working," Sonia told her with a pleased smile. "You've practically said so yourself."

"I . . . meant . . . with a boy," E.E. answered, feeling terribly self-conscious.

"I don't know why not," Sonia said. "It's hard for anyone to resist someone who is friendly and genuine."

But was she genuine? E.E. questioned herself as she lay in bed that night. She wanted to be, she really did. But how could she be certain?

The definition of genuine was the absence of pretense or affectation. What was pretense, the way she used to be or the way she was trying to be? One thing she did know: She felt a lot better about herself now, so evidently that supplied her answer.

Why not put Sonia's theory to the test? If she acted friendly and interested in Bruce, why shouldn't he start liking her again? The first thing she would have to do when she got the chance was apologize.

Maybe, just maybe, he would even ask her to the Harvest Ball. That really was far-fetched, but . . . but what was so impossible about it? Suddenly she realized it was something she wanted very much. She had just never let herself think about it before.

Snuggling down under the covers, E.E. let out a contented sigh and smiled happily to herself. Things didn't seem so impossible any more!

15

E.E. felt excitement bubbling up in her the moment she awoke Wednesday morning. For a few seconds she couldn't recall exactly why, and then she remembered. Today she was going to have a talk with Bruce if she got the opportunity.

"You look happy this morning," her mother commented when E.E. walked into the kitchen for breakfast.

"Happy," E.E. agreed, "but not hungry."

"And why not?" her mother demanded, frowning slightly.

"I can't help it, Mom. That's the way I always am when I'm excited."

"And what's happening today that's so exciting?" her mother asked, the frown changing into a smile.

"Well . . . nothing really," E.E. answered, taking the plate of bacon, eggs, and toast that her mother handed to her. "I just have this feeling that today is going to be special some way. Maybe the most important day of my life," she added in a melo-dramatic voice.

Her mother laughed. "My, that sounds awesome," she said, as she joined E.E. at the table with a cup of coffee. "You've really changed, honey, do you know that? Sometimes I hardly recognize you any more."

"Is that bad?" E.E. asked seriously, studying her mother's face. Was her mom trying to tell her something? She didn't look upset.

"On the contrary," her mother said, reaching over and patting her hand. "I think it's wonderful. You seem . . . oh, I don't know . . . so much more relaxed and sure of yourself, I guess. I like your friends, too, and it's nice to see you all having a good time."

"I'm glad you feel that way," E.E. said, as she toyed with her food. "You scared me there for a second. But, anyway, it's all your and daddy's fault."

"Why's that?"

"For shoving me out into the cold, cruel world and making me do something different for a change." Although E.E.'s voice was light and carefree, there was an underlying tone which was serious.

Her mother seemed to recognize that. "Then it's the best thing we ever did. And much easier than making you eat your breakfast," she added, glancing down at E.E.'s plate. "I hope you don't make yourself sick," she said, shaking her head in dismay.

"Missing one meal won't make me sick," E.E. answered with a laugh, standing and carrying her plate to the cabinet. She gathered up her books, put on her coat, and headed for the door. "Have a nice day," she called over her shoulder.

E.E. hoped she might see Cindy before first hour, but even though she waited at Cindy's locker for a long time, she didn't show up. She had probably gone to her locker when she first arrived at school and gotten what she needed then. Too bad—E.E. could use a little advice on how to talk to a boy.

She was becoming good friends with both Rita and Sheryl, and as the three of them were walking to the grade school that day, she realized they would be more than happy to give her advice as far as boys were concerned.

Both of them were pretty and popular, and had steady boyfriends. Still, they hadn't been friends long enough that E.E. could feel at ease talking to them about Bruce. It didn't matter, anyway, since they were busy talking about the Harvest Ball.

"Has anyone asked you to the dance yet?" Rita asked E.E. as they entered the grade school.

"No. I doubt if anyone will, either."

"Don't give up so soon," Sheryl said. "After all, it's still a month away, and some boys wait until the last minute to get a date."

"With the great dancing lessons we've been giving you, you'll be all set," Rita added.

"You've got to go to the Harvest Ball," Sheryl said as they entered the L.D. room. "That's one of the biggest dances of the year."

Lisa was sitting at the table closest to the door, and waved at E.E.

"If you want us to, maybe we could arrange a blind date," Sheryl said.

"I appreciate the offer," E.E. answered, "but I

don't think I'm ready to take such drastic measures. Thanks, though," she said as she went to join Lisa.

"All ready to get to work?" she asked Lisa in a cheerful voice.

Lisa's short hair bounced as she bobbed her head in answer to E.E.'s question. "When's the Harvest Ball?" she asked.

"You don't miss a thing, do you?" E.E. said with a laugh. "It's between Thanksgiving and Christmas."

"Don't you want to go?" Lisa whispered.

"Sure, if the right person would ask me," E.E. said, as she spread out some trace-the-number cards on the table in front of them.

"Like Bruce?" Lisa whispered again.

"Um-hum," E.E. murmured, nodding her head. She hadn't been paying that much attention to Lisa's question, but suddenly she realized just what she had answered. Looking around the room quickly, she discovered with relief that Bruce was sitting on the opposite side by the windows helping Tommy Jones.

She would have been mortified if Bruce had overheard them. Thank goodness Lisa didn't have any idea who Bruce was. She was going to have to be careful what she told Lisa in the future.

"No more questions," she stated firmly. "Let's see how well you can do today."

Lisa didn't do quite as well as she had the night before, but she was attentive and that was like crossing a major hurdle for her. Miss Kirkpatrick stopped by their table once and commented on Lisa's progress in the last few weeks.

When the class was over, E.E. told Sheryl and Rita

to go on without her. "I have something important I need to do," she explained.

Bruce was still sitting at his and Tommy's table putting some things away while the other boys walked out the door. This might be the best opportunity she would ever have to talk to him. Now or never, E.E. thought as she walked over to where he was.

"Something wrong, Elizabeth?" he asked as he scooted his chair back and stood up.

"Uh . . . not exactly," she murmured. "I was just wondering if . . . well . . . do you mind if I talk to you for a little while?"

"Fine," he answered. "I guess it will have to be on the way back to school, though."

"Sure, okay," she said as they walked to the door.

"What seems to be the problem?" Bruce asked once they were outside the building.

"It's not a problem, really," E.E. stammered, "but . . . well, yes . . . I guess it is. The problem's been me. I just wanted to apologize for how rude I was, and the way I've acted," she said in a rush. "I'm sorry, but I'm doing my best to change now." She couldn't bear to look at Bruce, but she felt like she had to. She held her breath as she slowly raised her eyes to meet his.

"Apology accepted," he said with a big grin.

He stuck out his hand and they shook, then they both laughed.

"I already knew you'd changed a lot," Bruce said in a serious tone. "This class has had a lot to do with it, hasn't it?"

"It really has," E.E. agreed as they walked along.

"But I'm not sure if it has been the class so much as Lisa."

"You didn't happen to be reading some books on Learning Disabilities when I saw you that Saturday in the library, did you?" Bruce asked with a twinkle in his eyes.

E.E. nodded, blushing. "How did you know?"

"It seemed the normal explanation when I thought about it later. So why did you run off the way you did after you put the books back?"

"Oh, uh . . . I suppose I had a guilty conscience over the way I'd been acting," E.E. said.

"I hope that's all, because now that's taken care of, we can be friends," Bruce said.

"I'd like that," E.E. answered with her warmest smile.

By now they had reached the high school. "See you tomorrow morning during Math Club," Bruce said as they headed in opposite directions.

Even though E.E. had skipped the first meeting of Math Club, she was really looking forward to the second meeting tomorrow. She felt almost like singing aloud from the sheer happiness rippling through her.

Elizabeth could hardly wait for school to be out. She was dying to talk to Cindy. Boys were crazy about her and she would be happy to give E.E. some advice and suggestions about Bruce, E.E. knew. Although she didn't plan to chase Bruce, it certainly wouldn't hurt to find out how to act around him.

As soon as physics was over, E.E. rushed to Cindy's locker.

"I'm glad you got here before I had to leave," Cindy said in a hurried voice.

"I thought you were riding the bus with me."

"I was, but something came up. I have to meet someone in town."

"Come over this evening, okay?" E.E. said. "I've got lots to talk about."

"You bet. It must be something neat."

"I'm not sure, but I hope it's going to be."

"I've got to go," Cindy said, looking at E.E. as if she would like to stay and hear more. With a quick good-bye and a wave, she hurried down the hall.

After Cindy left, E.E. went to her locker and gathered up her books. It was such lovely weather outside, she hated to think about riding the stuffy old school bus home.

The day had warmed up to almost sixty-five degrees. That was one thing about Oklahoma weather—you never knew what it would be like. It might be ten degrees one day and sixty-five degrees the next.

She could walk downtown and do some window shopping, have a Coke at the drugstore, then catch a city bus the rest of the way home. She was starting to get a little headache, and maybe the fresh air would help. Besides, she felt so elated and excited, she didn't know if she could sit still long enough to ride the bus.

Sonia's theory had worked! Bruce had responded when E.E. was friendly. He had said they were friends now, and there was no reason why things wouldn't keep getting better!

16

After giving her mother a call to tell her she would be a little late, Elizabeth started out. Although the weather was as warm and pleasant as a spring day, the trees were bare and the grass dry and brown.

How she wished it would snow before Christmas. For the short time snow remained on the ground here, it seemed to soften the stark landscape.

Since there was a Mr. Burger on the corner across from the high school, E.E. decided to stop there, get something to drink, and carry it with her.

She bought a large Coke and sipped it slowly as she walked along. Two blocks farther on, she passed Snuggle In. That was the hangout for many of the high school students and usually where Cindy went with her other friends.

E.E. could hardly wait until Cindy came over that evening. She had so much she wanted to talk to her about! Cindy would be able to give her all kinds of good advice about Bruce.

After E.E. had walked about half the distance to the business district of the city, she began to wish she had ridden the school bus. Instead of improving, her headache was feeling much worse. It seemed to throb and pound with each step she took.

Finally, she sat down on a sheltered bench and waited for the city bus. She would have to save the window shopping for another day, because she didn't feel like taking another step. All she wanted to do was take a couple of aspirin and lie down for a while.

It seemed like forever before a bus arrived, but one finally did. Climbing gratefully aboard, E.E. sat down on the nearest seat and leaned the side of her head against the cool window.

The bus turned the corner onto Dewey Street and passed Willow Creek Shopping Center. When it bumped across the railroad tracks, E.E. felt as if her head were being dragged across a washboard. Closing her eyes, she didn't open them again until the bus braked to a stop on the corner beside City Drug.

She was watching other passengers get off and on when she spotted a familiar figure out of the corner of her eye. Turning her head for a better view, E.E. gasped in surprise. Bruce Johnson stood by the door of the drugstore, holding it open as Cindy entered!

As the bus lurched forward, E.E. sat motionless, feeling as though she were in a state of shock. She could feel her enthusiasm drain away just as if someone had pulled a plug. She leaned back in the seat, letting her shoulders droop.

Then, slowly, her brain began to function clearly and she started thinking logically. It was only natural that this would happen. Cindy was such a sweet girl and she wasn't going steady with anyone, and Bruce was really a super guy. Cindy had said several times how she would like to date Bruce.

They would make a neat couple. She couldn't blame either one of them. After all, why should E.E. expect Bruce to like her when there was someone like Cindy around?

E.E. plopped her books down on the table as soon as she entered the kitchen.

"Hello, Mom," she said, the words sounding mechanical and lifeless.

"Are you all right, honey?" her mother asked, studying her face. "You look a little pale."

"I just have a headache, that's all," E.E. replied in a strained voice. Walking over to the cabinet by the sink, she took down the bottle of aspirin, shook out two, and swallowed them with a gulp of water. "I think I'll go lie down until it's time for dinner."

As soon as she was in her room, she flopped across her bed. It was going to take more than two aspirin to make her feel better, she thought sadly. She would have to put on a good act for Cindy so she would think E.E. was happy that she was dating Bruce.

Rolling over on her back, E.E. stared up at the ceiling. A lot of good it had done her to try and change! As soon as the thought hit her, she knew she couldn't allow herself to feel that way.

She wasn't going to fall apart and hide herself in her own little world like she had after the incident with Tom last spring. Thank goodness she was a bigger person than that now. She'd even come to realize that when Bruce asked out other girls earlier in the year, it hadn't meant that he couldn't like her at the same time.

She was really happy that Cindy and Bruce had gotten together, she told herself as two hot tears rolled out the corners of her eyes and trickled down the sides of her cheeks.

Surely there would be a special boy for E.E. some day, too. There was no law stating it had to be Bruce. It was just that . . . no other boy could ever measure up to him.

After dinner, which she barely picked at, E.E. decided to study for a trig test. Studying could usually take her mind off anything, but it didn't do the job this evening. Maybe because her head was still throbbing; but she knew that wasn't the reason.

She was sitting at her desk with her head bent over the book and her back to the door when Cindy called out in her bubbly voice, "Okay, I'm here! Now what was so important this afternoon?"

E.E. jumped in surprise, then turned around. She had forgotten all about Cindy's coming over this evening! What was she going to say? She certainly couldn't ask for any advice about Bruce now, and she didn't want to bring up seeing them together until Cindy was ready to tell her.

"Oh . . . it wasn't anything, really. It doesn't matter now," E.E. said.

"Of course it does," Cindy answered lightly. "I'm sorry I couldn't listen this afternoon, but I had some business to take care of."

"That's okay," E.E. said as Cindy sat down on the bed.

"So are you going to tell me what your news is, or not?"

"It was nothing . . . honest."

"Oh, E., I don't have time to pry it out of you now. I've got to run into town with Mom. If you change your mind, holler, okay?"

"Okay," E.E. answered as Cindy went out the door.

She was lucky that Cindy had to go with her mother. Cindy didn't give up easily and she would have pestered Elizabeth until she told her something.

Maybe it would work out best if E.E. were honest with her the way she had been with Bruce. Cindy might feel a little funny about going out with Bruce, and maybe E.E. should make the first move to let her know she didn't mind.

E.E.'s head was still pounding and she felt so miserable that she didn't even bother to take a shower. She changed into her pajamas and crawled into bed, drifting quickly into a troubled sleep.

When she awoke the following morning, she felt worse. She must have had a headache the day before because she was coming down with something. Now she was chilled, too, and every muscle in her body felt as though it were tied in knots.

When her mother took her to the doctor later in the day, he said her symptoms were those of a virus that was going around. She would have to stay in bed for a couple of days and take the medicine he prescribed.

It wasn't until Friday that E.E. even felt like sitting up in bed. She made a backrest of her two pillows and was leaning against them when her mother came in with a glass of Seven-Up and handed it to her.

"Cindy came by before school to see how you were," her mother told her. "She said she would come to see you when you felt better. And Lisa made Sonia Forrester call again to check on you."

"I wonder how Lisa got along today without me? I'll have to call her this afternoon and find out."

When it was time for Lisa to be home, E.E. walked out to the hall. After dialing the Forresters' number, she sat down on the carpeted floor and waited for an answer.

Mrs. Donnell, the lady who cleaned and cooked for the Forresters on weekdays, answered and in a few seconds Lisa was on the telephone.

"Beth, are you all right?" she asked, sounding as somber as if E.E. were in the hospital.

"I'm fine," E.E. said with a laugh. "I feel a lot better."

"Good," Lisa said, sounding like her old self.

"I'm sorry I couldn't help you last night or today."

"Me, too. I missed you."

"How did you do today?" E.E. asked.

"Okay," Lisa answered breezily. "I didn't hardly have to work."

"Didn't you have anyone to help you?" E.E. questioned.

"Yes, there was somebody," Lisa said. "Tommy Jones was sick, too, and the boy who usually helps him helped me instead. You'd never guess what his name was, either. It was Bruce, just like the name of the boy you like." Lisa giggled, then added, "This Bruce is nice, too."

"What did you study?"

"Oh, he didn't make me study much at all. We mostly talked."

"So . . . what did you talk about?" E.E. asked, feeling a little apprehensive about what Lisa's answer would be.

"You."

"M-me?" E.E. quavered, wishing that she had misunderstood and knowing that she hadn't. She could feel her heart starting to thump and bang against her ribs.

"Uh-huh," Lisa said.

"But what could you find to say about me?" E.E. asked. Her voice sounded weak and she held her breath as she waited for Lisa's reply.

"Oh, lots of stuff. Bruce just asked me if the girl who usually worked with me was nice, and I said, yes, next to my mom and dad you were the nicest person in the whole world."

"T-that's all, then?" E.E. asked.

"No. He wanted to know what was so special about you, so I told him about all the things you made to help me learn math and how you come over twice a week and help me. He thought that was super. I told him how we were both like butterflies, too. And guess what else?" Lisa asked in an excited voice.

"What?" E.E. bit her bottom lip and waited for the reply.

"He asked me if you have a boyfriend."

"Oh, no," E.E. moaned. "What did you tell him?"

"I said you didn't. But I told him that you like a boy whose name is Bruce, just like his. He thought that was funny, and he asked me what the other Bruce was like," Lisa rattled on.

E.E. didn't have the heart to ask Lisa any more, but she didn't need to, because Lisa was anxious to tell her everything she knew.

"I told him the other Bruce is real nice and that he sits behind you in physics, and that you wished he'd ask you to the Harvest Ball."

"Lisa! You didn't," E.E. moaned once more.

"Did I do something wrong?" Lisa asked in a worried voice.

"It's just that it's not always good to tell everything you know," E.E. explained, hoping she didn't sound as upset as she felt. "I've got to go now, but I'll see you Monday."

"I'm glad. Bye," Lisa chirped.

E.E. stood and hung up the phone, then sank down to the floor again and laid her head on her knees. How could she ever face Bruce Johnson again? If only there were some dark corner where she could go hide for the rest of her life. If she could even be sick for another week or so, it might help a little. Unfortunately, she was feeling much better physically.

If this had happened the other day, before she had seen Bruce and Cindy together, she probably would have been relieved that Bruce knew how she felt. But now she was certain it was the worst thing that could ever happen. How, oh how did she get into such predicaments?

17

Elizabeth got ready for school Monday morning with a feeling of dread. She planned to do her best to avoid Bruce today. She shouldn't have any trouble except for physics. Maybe by then she could figure out a way to come late and leave early.

E.E. was surprised at the reception she received when she arrived at school. Everyone she knew seemed happy to see her and welcomed her as if she had been absent a month instead of two days.

When it was time for activity period, Rita and Sheryl were waiting for her by the main door that they always left through.

"Hi," Sheryl said. "We missed you."

"Are you about ready for another dancing lesson?" Rita asked.

"Almost," E.E. answered. That was the last thing she felt like doing now, but she didn't want to let them know.

As they started down the sidewalk toward the

grade school, she was glad she was walking with the two girls. Not far ahead Bruce was walking slowly along by himself.

It didn't take long for them to catch up with him. The other two girls were chattering away and, thankfully, E.E. was in the middle. She turned to Rita and asked her a question as they passed Bruce. Anything so she could look in the other direction. Still, she could feel her face growing hot.

When they arrived at the L.D. room, Lisa was waiting for her right by the door.

"I'm so glad you're back," she said excitedly. "I sure did miss you. Bruce was nice, but not as nice as you. I bet he's nicer than the other Bruce, though. Why don't you like him instead?"

"Come on," E.E. said, grabbing Lisa's hand and walking quickly over to a table. There was no telling what Lisa might say next, and E.E. didn't want Bruce to walk in and hear her.

"That Bruce already has a girlfriend," E.E. whispered, "so don't talk about it anymore."

"B-but——"

"I mean it," E.E. said sternly. "Now let's see how well you can do today."

"Okay."

E.E. kept Lisa as busy as possible and didn't give her an opportunity to ask another question during the remainder of the class period.

When activity period was over, E.E. walked back to the high school armed with Rita and Sheryl on either side. So far, so good. Now she only had two more classes where she would see Bruce.

When it was time for trig, E.E. waited until the

last minute before she rushed into class. Everyone else was already in their seats. At the end of class, she was the first one up and out the door.

That meant she had to stall somehow until it was time for physics to begin, so she decided to take a long way around and come in at the last minute again.

I'm crazy, she told herself, as she walked slowly down the hall. But at least Bruce wouldn't think she was chasing him. Maybe, if she was lucky, he would even think that Lisa hadn't known what she was talking about last week.

When the warning bell rang, Elizabeth speeded up her steps. She stood by the door of the physics room until the last bell sounded, then darted into the door and walked to her seat.

It was hard to pass Bruce's desk without looking at him. More than anything else she would like to turn and give him a big, bright smile. He was one super guy even if he did like Cindy instead of her.

Instead, she kept her eyes riveted straight ahead. Still, she did catch a glimpse of his profile as she walked by. She held her books tightly to her chest as though they could stop the loud pounding of her heart. Here she was: seventeen years old, a senior in high school, and acting as if she were a sixth-grader with a crush.

It was the first time E.E. could remember that she couldn't concentrate during class. Having Bruce so near, knowing that he knew how she felt, and realizing that Cindy liked him, too, were just more than she could cope with.

It wasn't as if Bruce and Cindy were going steady.

They'd only had one date, but E.E. didn't want to do one thing to interfere. Not after the way Cindy had always been such a fantastic friend to her. Cindy deserved every opportunity to make this thing with Bruce work. E.E. was no competition, anyway, but she wanted to make sure Cindy knew she didn't mind.

Mr. Creason announced a test for Friday, which registered vaguely with her, but she didn't hear much of his lecture on induced currents, she was so busy with her own thoughts.

She was going to have to think of some way to get out of the room gracefully when class was over without having to see Bruce. If she once met his eyes, he would know that Lisa had told him the truth.

She hadn't handed in her make-up assignments—she could give them to Mr. Creason as soon as class was dismissed.

When the bell rang, she walked up to his desk and talked to him for a while. When she was finished, Bruce had already left for football practice.

E.E. felt about as energetic as a deflated balloon as she trudged down the hall to her locker. It was silly to feel so upset about losing something when it had never been hers in the first place, but she couldn't seem to help herself. The only thing she had to look forward to was fried chicken and apple pie for dinner that night.

Even that tasted like wood when she ate dinner that evening with her father and mother.

"You're not getting sick again, are you?" her mother asked, eyeing her with a worried look.

"No. I'm just not very hungry. Guess I'll save my pie for later," E.E. answered. She had taken one bite from it.

"I'll clean up in here," she told her mother when they were finished. "You go in the living room with Daddy."

"There's no reason for you to do it all alone," her mother protested.

"I want to," E.E. insisted.

After her parents left the room, she attacked the dishes as if working at full speed could take her mind off everything else. She had just finished putting away all the leftovers and loading the dishwasher when the doorbell rang.

A moment later her mother stuck her head in the kitchen door. "You have a visitor, honey," she said.

"If it's Cindy, Rita, or Sheryl tell them to come on in," E.E. said as she wiped off the counter. "I'm almost finished."

"It isn't, it's a boy," her mother whispered. "Just leave the rest and I'll finish."

Who could it be? E.E. wondered as she followed her mother into the living room. Whoever it was, her dad was talking about the last high school football game with him.

"Hello, Elizabeth," Bruce said, as she walked around the corner.

"B-Bruce," E.E. stammered. She could feel her cheeks growing as rosy as the strawberry-colored dress which she was still wearing.

"I hope you don't mind me dropping in like this," he said. "I thought maybe we could study for our physics test together."

"Well, yes, I'd like to," E.E. said, regaining some of her composure. What else could she tell him after her apology the other day? "Is it okay if I go to the library with Bruce, Dad?" she asked.

"Fine," her father answered, his eyes twinkling.

E.E. grabbed her coat out of the hall closet and put it on, all of the time feeling as if she were walking around in a dream.

"Ready?" Bruce said when she came back to join him.

She nodded mutely and he turned to her parents once more. "Will ten o'clock be too late, since this is a school night?" Bruce asked politely.

"That sounds about right," her father agreed.

E.E. could tell from the tone of her dad's voice that Bruce had already won his approval.

E.E. felt as though she were floating as they walked out the door and down the sidewalk to Bruce's car. This couldn't really be happening to her, not the very thing she had been hoping and wishing for. But there was still Cindy, and that thought was a nagging worry at the back of E.E.'s mind.

After they were in the car, Bruce studied her thoughtfully for a moment. Maybe he was wondering what he had gotten into. He was probably already regretting asking her to go with him.

"There's something we need to get straightened out right away," Bruce said in a serious voice.

"What's that?" E.E. asked, her voice squeaking slightly.

"I am *not* going to call you E.E.," Bruce said with a big grin. "I really don't care for Eureka, either. Elizabeth is all right, but Lisa said she calls you

Beth, and that's what I'd like to do, too. Do you mind?"

"I'd . . . like that," E.E. said, lowering her eyes. She just couldn't meet Bruce's gaze. For a while she had forgotten the part Lisa had played in this, but she couldn't forget any longer. Maybe that was the reason Bruce had asked her to go study, because of Lisa. "About Lisa," E.E. began, feeling terribly self-conscious.

"She's a super little girl," Bruce interrupted. "And very discerning. If it hadn't been for her, I might not have had the nerve to ask you out. I was afraid you didn't like me. Of course, I was beginning to hope again, after our little talk the other day."

The sincerity in Bruce's voice made a warm, contented glow spread through her, and she knew that a response wasn't necessary.

They rode for several blocks in a comfortable silence. But as they drove past the high school, E.E. remembered that she hadn't even brought her physics book along. Bruce was going to think she was a real nut.

"I forgot my physics book."

Bruce looked over at her, then began to laugh. "You'll never believe this," he said, "but so did I. I didn't even think about it and I'm the one who asked you to study with me. So what would you like to do?" he asked as he braked at a red light.

"We could go back to my house and study," E.E. suggested.

"Or," Bruce said, "we could go get a Coke some place and talk for a while."

"Fine."

"Where to?"

"We're close to City Drug," E.E. said. "Why don't we go there?"

"Sounds perfect, if you're sure you don't mind."

"Why should I——" E.E. began, then stopped abruptly. Of course! He was thinking about the first time he asked her to study at the library and have a Coke at the drugstore. That seemed like a million years ago, now. "Listen . . . about that first time you asked me to go study, I'll explain some time, okay?"

"You don't need to do that."

When they went into City Drug, E.E. was happy to see that there was only one other couple sitting in one of the booths. Bruce pointed out an empty booth isolated in a corner and they went over and sat down in it.

"I'm glad we came here," Bruce said, after he ordered them both a Coke. "We'll be able to hear each other talk, and I want to know all about you."

"I . . . wouldn't . . . know where to begin," E.E. said, blushing. She nervously stirred the ice in her Coke with her straw.

"We could start with Isaac Newton and Albert Einstein."

E.E. looked up quickly to see if Bruce was teasing, but she couldn't tell. The pleasant smile on his face could mean anything.

"Hey, I'm serious," he said, as if reading her thoughts. "That's one of the first things that attracted me to you—the biographies you were carrying the first day we bumped into each other. You wouldn't believe all the biographies I read this summer."

"Really?" E.E. asked, her curiosity piqued.

"Honest," he said. "Have you read any about Bertrand Russell?"

E.E. nodded and any shyness she had felt with Bruce vanished. They were soon talking as if they were lifelong friends, and E.E. could scarcely believe the things they had in common besides reading biographies.

Science and math were favorite subjects of them both, although they liked all the other subjects, too. When they got on the subject of English, E.E. discovered that Bruce was also writing his semester paper on Learning Disabilities, as she'd suspected when he was looking for the library books she had taken.

The time seemed to fly as they discussed school, music, parents, and colleges. It seemed as if they had only arrived at the drugstore when it was time to leave again.

"I had a great time," Bruce said when he walked E.E. to her door.

"So did I," she answered with her nicest smile.

"The only trouble is that we didn't get any studying done."

"Why don't you come over Wednesday, and bring your book this time?" E.E. asked with a laugh. "We can study here." The carefree sound of her voice surprised even her.

"It's a date," Bruce said with a big grin.

What have I done? E.E. asked herself as she got ready for bed a short while later. She had planned to stay out of Bruce and Cindy's way and now she was the one who had asked him to come over.

Evidently, Bruce was still dating different girls, trying to decide who he really liked. That was bad enough, but when the other girl was Cindy, that was too much!

18

When Elizabeth opened the front door for Bruce Wednesday evening, he waved his physics book at her with a flourish. "Look what I brought!" he said.

"Great," E.E. answered. "I have mine, too. I thought it would be nice to work out here," she said as she led him to the kitchen. "That way we'll be close to the snacks."

Bruce laid his book on the kitchen table, then hit his forehead with the palm of his hand. "Wouldn't you know?" he said. "I remembered my book, but I was going to stop and get a sack of doughnuts."

"It's a good thing you didn't," E.E. said with a grin. "You would have offended my mother, since that's exactly what she made today."

"Fantastic," he said as he sat down at the table and arranged his physics notes. "Let's see," he continued in a scholarly sounding voice. "Mr. Creason doesn't ask only obvious questions. We can ask each other those first, but then we need to really dig in and make sure we know everything else he might ask."

"It certainly sounds as if you're organized."

Bruce grinned at her and asked the first question as he tapped his pencil on the table. "Explain a magnetic line of force."

Just as he finished the question, the pencil bounced out of his hand and he and E.E. grabbed for it at the same time. As his hand touched hers, she could feel a tingling race up her arm. Talk about a magnetic line of force! Thank goodness Bruce couldn't read her mind, she thought as she told him the correct answer.

Finally, as they got into studying, she relaxed and felt at ease with him once more.

After they had studied and asked every question that even Mr. Creason could possibly think of, Bruce called for a break. "Let's try some of those doughnuts your mom made."

E.E. went to the refrigerator, took out a jar of apple cider, and poured two glasses. "Dad thinks there's nothing like cider with doughnuts," she explained as she heaped a plate with the freshly made rolls and sat it on the table.

"Especially homemade doughnuts," Bruce said as he came over and carried the glasses of cider for her.

When he had finished his third one, he leaned back in his chair and groaned. "Your mom is a good cook. Maybe we should study together more often."

After they finished their snack, Bruce helped her clean up the kitchen. They talked about the physics test and the L.D. class at the grade school, and then it was time for Bruce to leave.

Her parents had already gone to bed when E.E. and Bruce went into the living room. She took his coat out of the hall closet and walked with him to the front door. He put it on and smiled down at E.E.

"I had a nice time," he said. "Would you like to go to a movie Saturday evening? There's a good one playing at the Marshall Twin."

E.E. nodded her head, afraid to trust her voice. She was going to have to talk to Cindy, that's all there was to it, and find out exactly how Cindy felt about Bruce.

Cindy brought up the subject herself the next morning as they walked to the bus stop. "Listen, E., I can't be patient any longer. Why haven't you told me how things are going with you and Bruce?"

"I was going to, but, I was afraid you might. . . ." E.E. hesitated, hoping that Cindy would understand.

"Afraid I might what?" Cindy asked with a perplexed frown on her face.

"Well, I, uh . . . saw you and Bruce going into the drugstore together last Wednesday."

"He told me my advice worked. That's why I was getting tired of waiting for you to tell me."

"What advice?"

"He wanted to see me Wednesday to talk about you and find out if I thought you would date him. Naturally I said yes. Of course, you'd apologized to him by that time so he was already pretty confident."

Even though it was a cold, blustery day, E.E. suddenly felt as warm as if she were standing on a tropical beach. Bruce and Cindy had met to talk about her!

E.E. was certain that Saturday would never arrive. When it did, she spent the whole afternoon getting ready for her date with Bruce.

After she soaked in a bubble bath, she wrapped up in her fuzzy blue robe and called Cindy. A few minutes later, Cindy walked into her room.

"Your beauty consultant has arrived," she said in a dignified voice.

First they worked on her hair, and when it was perfect they started on the makeup.

"We don't want to overdo it," Cindy cautioned. "After all, the natural look is in and your skin is perfect as it is."

"I still have an hour," E.E. said when they finished.

"The movie doesn't start that soon," Cindy said.

"Bruce called this morning and asked if I'd like to go out for pizza first," E.E. explained, her eyes sparkling.

"Surely you didn't say yes?" Cindy said in a shocked voice.

"Why not?" E.E. asked, fearful that maybe she'd done the wrong thing.

"It's just hard to imagine, that's all," Cindy said with a giggle.

E.E. stuck out her tongue. "Seriously, though. How am I going to know if he really likes me?"

"He wouldn't ask you for a date if he didn't like you, silly."

"That's not what I mean. How will I know if he thinks I'm special and wants to keep dating me?"

"Don't worry. You'll know. Besides, he hasn't dated anyone else recently."

"Yeah, and what if I blow my first real date with him and he never wants to take *me* out again, either?"

"You blew everything at the very beginning, remember? And he still wants to date you."

"Thanks for reminding me," E.E. said in a woeful voice.

"Just pretend you're going to the library," Cindy said with a grin. "Now, I've got to go get ready for my own date."

After Cindy left, E.E. dressed in her denim skirt and a plaid Western shirt with a bolo tie, then paced the floor and worried about whether she was wearing the right thing. Cindy had assured her the outfit was perfect.

Really, what she was worried about, she realized as she sat down on the edge of the bed, was how Bruce felt about her. Was she just another girl to date, or did he like her as much as she did him?

E.E. stared unseeingly at the wall of her bedroom. When the doorbell rang, she hopped up from the bed, grabbed her jacket and purse, and walked into the living room.

Just the mere sight of Bruce, tall and handsome standing by the door talking to her parents, made her heart turn flip-flops. He was wearing jeans and a Western shirt almost identical to her own. At least she wouldn't have to worry about her clothes any more.

"You look great, Beth," he said, taking her jacket and holding it for her as she slipped her arms in.

"Thanks," she murmured. His eyes held hers for a

magic moment and her mind whirled with the phrase, "magnetic line of force."

By the time they arrived at the Pizza Hut and found a place to sit, all of E.E.'s nervousness had vanished.

Bruce had just finished ordering a medium, super-supreme pizza when they heard a shrill voice call their names. "Beth, Bruce . . . hi!" Lisa ran over from the table where she had been sitting with her family and stood looking at them.

"Hi, yourself," E.E. said.

"Are you on a date?" Lisa asked Bruce.

"You better believe it."

"I knew you'd keep your promise," Lisa said. "Are you going to ask Beth to the Harvest Ball, too?"

E.E. could feel her face flushing with embarrassment as Bruce leaned over and whispered something in Lisa's ear.

"Okay," Lisa answered softly. "Bye," she said, waving at E.E., then dashing back to her family.

"I'm . . . sorry about Lisa," E.E. stammered.

"She's just a little overly enthusiastic at times," Bruce said with a warm grin. "Don't worry about what she said, either. I've been looking forward to dating you from the first time we crashed into each other, and the only reason I promised her I would take you out was because I wanted to do it."

"That part didn't bother me."

"Don't worry about the other. I want you to have a nice time tonight."

When they climbed in the car about an hour and a half later, Bruce didn't start the engine immediately. "We have plenty of time to get to the movie," he said, "and I want to ask you something."

"Sure," E.E. answered.

"Will you go to the Harvest Ball with me?" He lifted her hand, which was resting on the seat, and held it in his large one. E.E.'s hand seemed to tingle from his touch and she wished that he would go on holding it forever.

"Thank you, Bruce, but please don't feel . . . that because Lisa. . . ."

"Lisa has nothing to do with the way I feel about you, and don't forget it. You're just the kind of girl I've wanted to date. At first, I thought I might have made a mistake and maybe you were just an intellectual snob. But you weren't. The real you was there all the time, just like I'd hoped."

"In that case, I would love to go," E.E. answered, a smile on her face.

"Want to know what I whispered to Lisa tonight?" Bruce asked softly.

"What?"

"I told her, yes, I was going to ask you to the Harvest Ball, but it had to be at a special time because you were such a special girl."

"Oh, Bruce," E.E. whispered, her heart pounding loudly in her ears.

He moved toward her and all E.E.'s thoughts stopped as his lips covered hers. They were warm and sweet and gentle as he kissed her tenderly. Then he scooted back behind the steering wheel and patted the seat beside him.

"Why don't you sit here next to me? I kind of like your company."

"Okay," she answered, sliding across the seat to sit closer.

When their eyes met and held once more, E.E. realized Cindy was right. *I like him so much, and I* know *he feels the same way about me.* She felt as light and carefree as a butterfly, and somehow she felt certain that her metamorphosis was complete.

About the Author

Sandy Miller lives and works on a boys'
ranch in Oklahoma with her husband
and six children. She is also the author of
TWO LOVES FOR JENNY, available in
a Signet Vista edition.

Bestsellers from SIGNET VISTA